LIFER

LIFER

A NOVEL

JOHN RHEA

REDHAWK
PUBLICATIONS

ISBN: 978-1-959346-74-6 (Paperback)
Library of Congress Control Number: 2025930746

Book Layout: Robert Canipe and Erin Mann
Book Cover Photo: May Rhea; Cover Layout: Erin Mann
Author Photo: Lucy Cobos

Printed in the United States of America
First printing 2025.

Redhawk Publications
The Catawba Valley Community College Press
2550 Hwy 70 SE
Hickory, NC 28602
https://redhawkpublications.com

For May

In Memory of HHS

It was the epoch of uneasy alliances.

— Thomas McGuane, *Ninety-Two in the Shade*

Chapter 1

Everyone in our Unit has a nickname. It's another feature of prison that's reminiscent of high school, along with boredom, bullying, racial animosity, and sexual frustration. Congaree Correctional Institution is a microcosm of societal ills. Sadly, many of these kids are barely out of high school. But they make a big production of acting like they're tough guys with their swaggering and taunting. Lesson #1: You'd better be able to back that shit up.

Some of them are just punks who will fight only if they're part of a pack. Such posturing is necessary when you're under the constant threat of violence. Most aren't stupid, just undereducated. They may mangle the Queen's English, but I am frequently amazed by their situational awareness as well as their extensive knowledge of what interests them—cars, sports, music, supermodels, interests I generally share with them. But the most important thing we have in common is the fear that, barring some legal miracle, we're all going to die in this place. Usually it's the young guys who can't face this brutal fact. That's when desperation sets in, and desperate prisoners are dangerous to themselves and to others. They disrupt the orderly, day-to-day functioning of what, in essence, is a monastic existence that I and others have resigned ourselves to.

Easy Ed, our resident wit, is responsible for coming up with nicknames. He understands that a little levity is essential in an environment otherwise filled with hopelessness and regret. He takes his task seriously, striving for accuracy and originality. He has named Torch, Panic, Skunk, Lars, Scripts, and Master, whose last name is Bates, of course. Self-pleasure seems his only pastime. There's also Big C and Scuzz and Fleet, a former gang member with a gunshot-related limp. Even the guards get one: Hawk, Troll, Beef, and Ditto, a nervous rookie who repeats whatever his superiors say.

My nickname, predictably enough, is Counselor because I was once a criminal defense attorney—search no further for irony. I have done my best to use my knowledge to help other inmates who've asked for assistance. I initiated a state court appeal for Skunk and a complex federal *habeas corpus* for Torch that required months of research, despite knowing that neither of these efforts has the slightest possibility of success. Since my legal advice is now deemed indispensable, I am protected by Lars and Torch, collectively known as the Firm.

Just last week, Lars intervened when a guy named Primo tried to steal my food, not that it was worth fighting over. Primo now takes Fleet's food instead. More importantly, the Firm does not allow Scuzz to threaten to make me his bitch anymore. Torch, a black bodybuilder with arm tattoos of fire that accentuate his massive biceps, is without question the most feared man in the Unit. I was present when Torch told Scuzz that he'd cut off his dick and shove it down his throat if Scuzz ever messed with me. I've never been so glad to hear something in my whole life.

We are a diverse group in Unit 4, as our varied nicknames suggest. But we have all been convicted of murder and are therefore isolated from the general prison population. We have to get along with one another or else face solitary, which some men consider worse than anything other than the Needle. We are not death row, that's Unit 7. Sometimes people go crazy in solitary without the comfort of another inmate to talk to. Evidently, just listening to the voice inside their head all day is unsettling. I can relate.

The person I most enjoy talking to is Miguel Escovedo, the prison chaplain, or the Padre, as the men call him. Miguel is a kind and earnest man of seventy with whom I have thought-provoking theosophical discussions. He is committed to challenging my atheism and sees me as a potential candidate for conversion, albeit a difficult one. Miguel is self-conscious about his bad teeth and any time I make him smile, he quickly covers his mouth with his hand. I do not mean to make my friend uncomfortable, but I also enjoy making him laugh. So, it is a quandary.

Miguel brings me books that would otherwise be impossible to get, for which I am very thankful. Last time he brought a collection of Chekhov's short stories, without which I might've gone insane. I never fully appreciated the brilliance of a story such as "Ward No. 6" until I was incarcerated. These times demand somber stories. Unfortunately, Miguel visits only twice a month, so I'll have to wait to get something else good to read.

One reason my relationship with Miguel means so much to me is that I don't have family who visits anymore. My parents have long since passed and my estranged wife, Emily, moved to New Mexico last year to pursue her dream of becoming a working artist. My nephew, Stephen, came to see me when I was first sentenced, but then he moved to California. I have no relationship with Stephen's mom, my sister Rachel, and I have no children. Other than Emily and, occasionally, my lawyer, the only person who still writes to me is my cousin Gil, who was my co-defendant. Gil is also serving a life sentence, but he's housed in the lower part of the state because the South Carolina Department of Corrections does not allow co-defendants to be incarcerated in the same facility for fear of reprisals. I read his letters but I will never respond because I cannot forgive him, although at one time we were like brothers. Our mothers were fraternal twins. Gil is four years older and I worshipped him growing up. Love of family once sustained me. But now there's nothing, just memories before this nightmare began.

It troubles Miguel that I no longer have any association with family. I'll read portions of Gil's letters to him, things that aren't too personal or irreverent, so Miguel will have some idea of how intelligent Gil is and how well he can write. Once, not so long ago, he was a talented journalist and short story writer. As far as I know, he hasn't been able to get anything published since his confinement. I also want Miguel to see how manipulative Gil can be, how persuasive with his convoluted logic, how careless and narcissistic. I want Miguel to see how I was roped in.

Gil's letters make Miguel laugh more than my jokes do. I point out to him that this very fact shows the power of Gil's personality. Miguel now seems ashamed to laugh at the letters but he can't help himself. Gil may well have a touch of genius, but this gift is ruinous to those who come into his orbit.

Miguel has often suggested that I share my story in hopes it will be therapeutic. To date, I have resisted the idea. But news from the infirmary this week has changed my thinking. The doctor said that I am in good health for a male of fifty-two years. My life, and therefore my sentence, is liable to be a long one. It's not the news I was hoping for or, frankly, expecting, given decades of alcohol abuse and chain-smoking.

"You must have good genes," the young doctor stated as he hurriedly closed the manila folder, eager to leave the prison. Good genes? Two cousins are lifers for homicide, but the family DNA is healthy. Go figure. In light of this, I decided to survey the map of my life and search for all of the wrong turns, examine the critical miscalculations, and probe the numerous character flaws that landed me in Congaree. If you've never met Gil, I doubt you'll buy my excuses. As my sentencing judge said, disapprovingly, "Mr. Merritt, you had all of the advantages in life, and look at how you squandered them."

Chapter 2

No natural light reaches our subterranean unit. We are allowed outside on the yard for only one hour a day, which is not enough for any living creature, not even felons. Albinos in orange, we white boys have become accustomed to our institutional pallor. Inmates are not allowed to wear sunglasses (Regulation 42(g)), so we cover our eyes and squint like coal miners emerging from their shift. Not a day goes by—and they pass slowly—that I don't miss the sunlight and uninterrupted play of my youth. Increasingly, I move toward those memories, however painful they are.

I really don't know how to start my story. A powerful opening line hasn't come to me in the middle of the night, other than, say, "I fucked up," a common refrain in any prison. Every time I think of possible beginnings, a single image appears, an image, perhaps, because my wife is a painter. Back when we were happy, Emily and I spent every vacation traveling to art museums all over the world. Her idea, not mine. What little I know of art and art history, I learned from her. Painters understand that slight color changes can transform emotions. But you must perceive them. Many times I couldn't, at least not without Emily's help.

She was perceptive in other ways. Years ago she predicted that my blind allegiance to Gil would one day lead me into trouble. "Just because Gil refuses to grow up doesn't mean *you* have to," Emily said. "That *enfant terrible* bullshit is wearing thin. He's not a grad student, for God's sake!" She was concerned that, with Gil as a running partner, I would get a DUI or a minor drug charge or get involved in a bar fight, something that might even ruin my legal career. She understood Gil's temperament all too well, although even she could not imagine that my misplaced loyalty would have such dire consequences.

For Emily's birthday one year, I transformed our garden shed into an artist's studio. I enlarged two windows to capture the morning sun and fixed the place up with some comfortable furniture and a fancy wine rack. My gift delighted her, and her output, mostly oils, some pastels, increased considerably. On one of the walls, she framed a Monet quote: "It's on the strength of observation and reflection that one finds a way. So we must dig and delve unceasingly."

In the mental image I keep seeing, I am twelve years old. I have just unsaddled my first horse, Jed, after a vigorous ride. The fading October light glints off his sweaty black coat. The importance of the memory is simply this: I was content. Later, corrosive envy changed everything. At fifteen, I realized that, through no fault of my own, I would always be compared unfavorably to someone I loved and respected. Gil was smarter, more athletic, better looking, and wittier, assets counterbalanced by recklessness, vanity, and delusions of grandeur. For me, it was like hitting a tennis ball against a practice wall and waiting for the wall to make a mistake. I could never match up.

To be clear, I was not made to feel this way by my parents, both of whom were supportive. My sense of inferiority was fueled by watching how others interacted with Gil, whether family, friends, acquaintances, or strangers, for my cousin *commanded* a room as few others could. He possessed a hypnotic charisma that could turn the most strong-willed into followers before they were even aware of it. And he knew it. When Gil looked women in the eye, they usually believed what he said, no matter how preposterous it might be.

To his credit, Gil was enough of a romantic in his twenties to resist marrying the aluminum foil heiress from Vassar who was obsessed with him. He could have enjoyed a stress-free financial existence working for his father-in-law but Gil chose otherwise. I remember when he brought her home once for a Christmas visit. She was pretty and not snobbish, at least to our faces, but it was obvious to the whole family that he didn't love her.

I still believe that he never knew why he left New York to move back home to South Carolina. Sometimes he said it was to help with writer's block. Other times he mentioned money and homesickness. In any case, it was a mistake. He should've just stayed there, worked odd jobs, and finished his novel. Earlier, he described his work-in-progress as "close to completion," and years later, as "stillborn." In his most recent prison letters, he once again sounds positive about the novel. I wonder if he expects me to be happy for him.

Chapter 3

When we were kids, Gil and I spent many happy hours at our grandparents' farm, which was situated along the rocky banks of the Catawba River about six miles outside our hometown of Warrington. It was always exciting to leave behind our claustrophobic, cookie-cutter neighborhoods and head out to the country. Our mothers grew up on the farm and had a special reverence for the property, as did their children. My maternal grandfather, a textile executive, realized his life's goal when he was finally able to buy back the seven-hundred acre tract that had fallen out of family hands in the twenties because of a relative's gambling debts. On it he built a Georgian-style house that could accommodate weekend hunting parties, as if we were landed gentry.

Gil and I enjoyed barefoot childhoods at the farm. In those days, parents were less protective of their kids and we were free to roam the property at will, like Tom and Huck. The farm was sacred ground. We swam, fished, rode horses, built forts and tree houses, and almost blinded each other with slingshots and BB guns. We raced canoes all over the river, oftentimes crashing on the shoals, but always acquiring more knowledge about the rhythms of the rushing water. On horseback, we tried to chase deer and turkey off the property so that they would be safe from hunters. Livid when he discovered this, Grandad threatened to revoke our horse privileges, but Gran, our grandmother, interceded. It was she, after all, who had inspired our quest with her stories about a futuristic world in which all animals are spared.

Once, unexpectedly, Gil and I saw a sleek, muscular black panther drinking at the south creek, this before the game wardens ever believed they'd come up from Florida. I was seven and it was the first time I was terrified. We were about thirty yards away and could see its sculpted crouch as it drank from the stream. Gil could tell I was shaking and put his hand on my shoulder, signaling me to remain still and quiet. The panther, sensing something, effortlessly uncoiled, jumped the creek, and disappeared into the woods on the opposite side. Its speed, both awe-inspiring and frightening, emphasized just how vulnerable we were had it chosen to attack us. Frantic, I started running back to the house a half-mile away. Though much faster, Gil ran protectively behind me the whole way, looking over his shoulder to see if we were being pursued.

"We're okay," he kept assuring me. "It's not coming, Jack. You're all right."

When we arrived at the house, I was almost hysterical. Our typically skeptical grandad was convinced that we had merely seen "one of those little bobcats." It was not until there were reports of similar sightings on neighboring farms that we were vindicated, an article in the local newspaper mentioning us by name as witnesses to its existence. Gil would later fictionalize this incident in one of his first collegiate short stories, which was very accomplished for a nineteen year old.

Two years later, Gil actually would save my life. We were riding on the farm and my horse Toby's hoof hit a nest of yellow jackets. When I yelled, Gil took off on his horse, unscathed. Toby got stung, reared up, and threw me. I was quickly swarmed. I ran as fast as I could, but no nine year old ever outran a squadron of angry yellow jackets. When Gil realized I was on foot, he circled back around to help me. By that time, my throat had already begun to close and my breathing was labored. As I went into anaphylactic shock, I began to vomit. I had never been stung before and didn't know that I was allergic, but Gil realized I needed immediate medical attention.

Even now, I still marvel at what he was able to do. He heaved me over his shoulder and then mounted his horse. I recall his arm wound tightly around my legs and my chin bouncing off of his back as we galloped at top speed toward the house. If Gil had dropped me, I probably would've broken my neck.

I have a vague memory of my mother driving me to the emergency room, talking in a slow, calming cadence that was incongruous with the high speed at which we were traveling: "Breathe slowly. Take your time, baby. Just relax. Breathe. You'll be fine. That's it." I also recall the sound of her fingers tapping nervously on the steering wheel.

My dad wasn't able to get the smell of puke out of the car and sold it weeks later. I couldn't go anywhere without my new EpiPen. And from that day forward, I owed Gil big time.

Not all days on the farm were that exciting. Back then, we were allowed to do what most kids today are not—nothing. Our long summer days had no schedule. Gil and I ambled about with our dogs, just playing fetch, wading creeks, or if we felt ambitious, raiding Grandad's garden for a tomato. We also spent a good deal of time lying around in green fields, staring up at cumulus clouds through the sturdy limbs of two-hundred-year-old oaks.

Before discovering girls, we had decided that the most fun you could have was riding horses accompanied by your dogs. The interplay among three species while moving at a high rate of speed is a singular joy, and one that I continued to experience as long as I was a free man. I often dream about the sensation of a horse accelerating underneath me as it shifts from a lope to a gallop. The only thing I dream about more is being with Emily. Before I went to prison, I gave my two walkers, Scout and Midnight, back to the man in Tennessee from whom I'd bought them eight years before. I trusted him. He had been genuinely shocked by my reversal of fortune.

It is a testament to our connection with the farm that Gil and I chose to bury our childhood dogs there rather than at our homes in town. In the country, they were free to run. Quincy, Gil's golden retriever, and Charlie, my Old English Sheepdog, were best friends and are buried beside each other on a hillside overlooking the house, their graves marked by large mounds of fieldstone that Gil and I gathered without the help of the adults.

I went there on my final visit to the farm before my court appearance, the stones covered with acorn shells left by squirrels. When I spooked a red-tailed hawk in a pine tree, he rose to another vantage point. As the sky grew dark and the air cooler, I could see threads of fog curling around trees along the edge of the woods. I remembered Charlie's penchant for corn on the cob, which made me smile. For some reason, I put business cards on both dogs' graves. I glanced at the house and realized that I'd left a light on in an upstairs bathroom. I walked down in darkness to unlock the door for the last time.

Three days later, the farm was lost to me. And I was no longer Jackson Merritt, Esquire. I had become Department of Corrections # 275839.

§

Once the Unit goes dark, I remain awake. I can occasionally hear Master snoring before he turns over on his stomach, but that's about the only distraction. The quiet is a welcome change. Days are loud and bustling. On Tuesday, out of boredom, I counted 163 "fucks" uttered by my fellow inmates and the guards. Panic was the clear winner. At night, when all of the anger and frustration gives way to silence, it comforts me to remember the sounds of the farm: barred owls calling on a full moon, cicadas in symphonic waves, Grandad's hunting dogs baying, deer rustling in the fields, bullfrogs and peepers by the pond, and January winds wailing across the river.

And the smells. You would be hard-pressed to find a fouler human environment than Unit 4 with its stench of urine, sweat, mold, mildew, and something resembling rotting cheese. I haven't determined the source of this smell yet, but on my worst days I'm convinced it's nothing less than the decay of men's hope. On the verge of sleep, I recall newly cut hay, horse sweat, blackjack soil, spawning bream, pasture grass after a good rain, honeysuckle in summer, and wood smoke in winter. All of this remembrance of things past doesn't make up for sharing the nightmares of condemned men, but it helps.

Chapter 4

Scripts has a new mule. The last one got busted and is currently doing time. The poor thing remained steadfast in her story that she was attempting to surprise Scripts with a delivery and he knew nothing about the drugs. Chivalry being dead, Scripts refused to help her out because he hates going to the hole. The vindictive prosecutor persuaded the judge to give the girl a year, plenty of time to contemplate her decision. She had no prior record, according to Scripts. I can't imagine where he finds these women, or what's in it for them.

Scripts is that guy we all knew in high school who boasted about doing more drugs than anybody: "I make Keith Richards look like the Pope!" He says "man," "dude," and "cool" too often. But he is also a shrewd capitalist and lets it be known that he can hook you up with whatever you want. Though he has a few competitors, Scripts is by far the most proficient importer of narcotics in the Unit. Short but cocky, he has a cadre of sycophants, some so strung out on opioids that they're physically dependent on the success of Scripts' business enterprise. Their moods fluctuate dramatically based upon the availability of certain chemicals.

Most pharmaceuticals and marijuana enter the prison in a janitorial delivery truck. The drugs are distributed by Scripts' contacts in shipping and receiving. A guy who tried to skim off the top was found badly beaten, lying by a dumpster near one of the bays, too afraid to snitch. Heroin, LSD, crack, and meth usually come in through mules or the occasional prison employee on the take. The term "maximum security" is somewhat misleading, although it's true that no one has ever escaped from Congaree Correctional.

There was one fatal heroin overdose in the Unit this past year, a middle-aged man with whom I'd never spoken. It's inexcusable that I can't remember his nickname right now. His death was ruled a suicide (a handwritten note addressed to his teenage daughter was found by the bed) and the subsequent investigation quickly ended. Once again, Scripts went unscathed. Like any successful dealer, his money allows him to enjoy the best of what our environment has to offer: expensive food from the canteen so he doesn't have to eat cafeteria slop, state-of-the-art headphones, a sizable collection of pornographic materials, the occasional cell phone to facilitate importation, and at least one guard on his payroll. Even the Firm doesn't have that kind of clout.

Almost everyone has partaken of Scripts' contraband, myself included. It used to be that the only safe place to smoke pot was on the yard, but with the advent of edibles you no longer have to worry about the guards getting a whiff. I get mine directly from Easy Ed, who understands my desire for secrecy, seeing as I am the in-house counsel for Unit 4. I can't have my credibility called into question. Last month I foolishly spent all of my canteen money on dope. Ed swears he's not making a profit off me and I believe him. Scripts is expensive. Such easy access to ganja has transformed my prison experience for the better since I am markedly less depressed whenever I'm stoned.

When I got to prison, the doctor immediately prescribed Zoloft, then Paxil, but both antidepressants made me feel worse, which I didn't think was possible. There is no greater torment than simultaneously feeling suicidal and yet afraid to finish the job, to end the unimaginable minute-by-minute suffering and the fucking insomnia that goes with it. Sleep deprivation alone is torture enough. My decision to go with herb was an easy one.

The inevitable stoner apathy that is so ridiculed on the outside is actually quite helpful in prison. I've found that it pairs nicely with sitting alone in an 8-by-8 concrete cell for endless hours. Eventually boredom, tedium, and routine become your friends, and you realize that daydreaming can be perfected into a minor art form, a kind of personal theater. On the downside, Miguel has noticed that I occasionally have short-term memory lapses, and starting out, there were times when I miscalculated the dosage and the ensuing paranoia crippled my thinking. This stuff is definitely not the ragweed Gil and I used to smoke growing up. I'd sit crouched in the corner drooling, pondering the innumerable bad things that lurked outside my cell. Through trial and error, I now have a better handle on it, discovering that half a gummy does the trick.

I've never been caught. Once an inmate receives three minor drug infractions, he has to go to the hole. As a rule I'm very careful, but even if I went to solitary, it wouldn't be the end of the world. They can't deny you food and drink there. I would just read *Crime and Punishment* again. In retrospect, it probably would have been a good idea to read it before coming to prison, but somehow, with my busy law practice, I never had the time.

I normally find out about Scripts' activities through hearsay. In the cafeteria at lunch, some of the guys are gathered around talking about Scripts' latest venture. Panic, who's on prescription meds for his anxiety disorder, is supplementing those pills with something from Scripts that makes him even more hyperactive. He constantly drums his fingers on the plastic food tray, which is very annoying. Master, now in his late 30s, retains traces of his rebellious youth in Myrtle Beach. He has a cobra tattoo coiled around his neck and earlobe piercings through which you could easily slide a No. 2 pencil. He sees himself as Scripts' emissary. He and Panic gossip more than bored retirees at a country club. Skunk, Easy Ed, and I listen in.

"My boy Scripts wants to have a party on his birthday," Master says. "And the party favor is blotter. Everybody's gonna get a hit on the house."

"She's bringin' it in her cootie," Panic says.

"I thought the last one tried that," Skunk says.

"Well, things went a little haywire. Timing is everything," Master says.

"Yeah, that girl's timing now," Easy Ed points out.

"Man, he never asked that chick to take the fall," Panic says. "She done it on her own 'cause she was in love with him. You should check out them letters she wrote him. They're so fuckin' dirty I got a hard-on reading 'em." He grins, exposing a gaping black hole where a tooth used to be.

"Bet he hasn't got any love letters since she went to jail," Ed says.

"I sure hope the new girl's better looking than that last chick," Skunk says. "Thinking about how nasty she was kinda spoiled my appetite for the drugs."

"You one to talk. Your old lady was no Miss Universe," says Panic.

"I'm sure it'll be packaged up nice and tight, boys. With a little balloon for wrapping," Master says confidently, taking his last bite of a rubbery slice of bologna.

"Why does Scripts think this mule will work?" I ask.

"Cause it's all about the information, Counselor. See, you gotta have the information in the modern world." He winks at me. I can tell he's quoting someone.

"I see."

"I thought you said it was all about timing," Skunk says.

"It's the same thing in this case," Master says. "Turns out Scripts is friendly with one of the female officers, one of 'em who isn't a dyke. I think her name's Wanda. The one with big tits." Master pauses to take a drink of tea. "Wanda don't like to do the cavity search. She ain't into that shit *at all*. Not like Joyce and them other field hockey players. Wanda likes dick. Same as Panic." Loud laughter. Panic pushes Master's shoulder good-naturedly.

"What we found out is..."

"We who?" Ed interrupts. He would've made a good lawyer.

"What *Scripts* found out," Master continues, "is that Wanda only checks a pussy when her superiors are around. Other times she lets it slide." I can't help but wonder what Scripts would think about a member of his posse being so indiscreet with such vital intelligence.

"Scripts knows all, man. It's his world, we just live in it," Panic says.

"Yeah. This girl Wanda just happens to be doin' a solo shift next Friday. None of the other guards will be anywhere in sight. I'll let you guess what day is Scripts' visitation," Master says with a satisfied smile.

"That's a thing of beauty there," Skunk says.

"Genius, ain't it?" Panic says, elbowing Ed's arm.

"Listen, dumbshit, you don't end up in here if you're a fucking genius, okay," says Ed.

Two guards, Beef and Ditto, walk into the cafeteria from the east corridor and we all return silently to our food trays. In a low voice, Master says, "Let's hope Scripts' birthday is like fuckin' Woodstock."

Then Beef announces: "All right ladies, this ain't no picnic. Wrap it up!"

"Picnic's over, men," Ditto says. "It's seven o'clock on the dot."

Panic gazes at Ditto, then shakes his head in a theatrical, exasperated manner and whispers, "What is it makes me wanna punch that kid's fuckin' face?"

"His voice," Skunk says.

"His face," Master says.

"Uh...maybe because you're a psychopath?" Easy Ed says.

Across the gymnasium-sized cafeteria, other guards herd groups of inmates down chutes leading to the four cell blocks. The cafeteria is the hub of Unit 4. All corridors lead to this, the home of tasteless food and conversation.

Constructed in 2010, Congaree embodies the latest innovations in large-scale human warehousing, its functionality exceeded only by its sterility. Even the TV/rec room has less personality than a Greyhound bus station—no murals, no pictures, just rows of uncomfortable plastic chairs bolted to the floor. A ton of taxpayer money has been spent on this impregnable fortress in order to ensure the safety of the citizenry, so I guess that when the nukes start flying, there will be nothing left of civilization but us felons and some bunkered preppers in Montana.

Per procedure, we are all handcuffed to waist chains before being escorted to cell block D. Beef handles this task while Ditto stands to the side, resting his right hand on his Taser like a gunfighter. I'm pretty sure he's just nervous and not trying to intimidate us, although Panic would disagree with that assessment. On the way down the corridor, we joke around with Beef, who's one of our favorite guards because he has a sense of humor, treats us respectfully, and is gentle with the cuffs. He knows they hurt.

"How's Mrs. Beef doing?" Ed asks.

"She thinks she's won the lottery gettin' to sleep with me. You know what I say: 'Once you try fat, you know where it's at.' She wouldn't have anything to do with a skinny fucker like you, Edward," Beef says.

"I'm sure her good cooking would fatten me up pretty quick. Please tell Gladys how much we appreciate everything she does. Those damn sugar cookies were delicious," Ed says.

"I'll do it. I should have some brownies on Thursday."

"Holy shit," says Panic, "Those are my fuckin' favorite. Tell her I said thanks, would ya?" Panic is a man who shot a bank security guard five times in the face in a botched robbery attempt.

"Yeah, she's a special lady. You might wanna hold on to her, big guy," says Skunk, who killed his boss at the bottling plant after years of heated disagreements.

"Beefy, I'm in love with your wife. And I plan on marrying her just as soon as I beat this bum rap and get the fuck outta here," says Master, whose two drug-related murders were neither bum raps nor beatable offenses.

"Gotta warn you, Master. She's not a fan of piercings or tattoos. Thinks they're the sign of the Devil," Beef says.

"She's probably right," Master says. "But when the love is real, you can get past a lot."

"Did I ever mention she's bigger than me?" Beef says. In a rare show of emotion, Ditto snickers. I'm glad to know he's not a total flatliner. The rookie will need to develop a good sense of humor in here.

Beef's wife has been sending us baked goods from her kitchen for six months now. Technically, this is a violation of Regulation 17, which prohibits gifting between staff and inmates. But it's one of the rules that gets bent with Hawk's tacit permission. As the head guard and someone who's enrolled in a night class on criminology, Hawk no doubt realizes that this benevolent gesture is good for morale. Or he may have reasoned that the worst thing that can happen is some prisoner will use a cookie to poison a pedophile. Gladys's treats are always accompanied by Southern Baptist literature containing hopeful, redemptive Bible verses.

The corridor narrows into a hallway. We arrive at a steel door labeled 426. Beef and Ditto stand behind us. Beef pushes the intercom button and talks into the wall: "Sergeant Benfield at 426 with 5 inmates." He is following protocol to the letter. We are on surveillance video. If something is wrong, a hostage situation, for example, Beef is to use a coded message. Somebody said it involves the phrase "en route," but I haven't confirmed this. I do know that whoever is in the control room can clearly see every one of us from multiple angles. There are no blind spots. The State spared no expense on technology. Master control uses a touchscreen computer to allow entry. Within seconds, the latch on the door's electrical locking mechanism retracts with a metallic thunderclap. The hallway narrows. We now walk single file. In twenty yards, we come to door 427. The process is repeated. It'll be the same with door 428, at which point we will enter an expansive control room beside the cell block. This stretch between 426 and 428 is claustrophobic and eerily quiet. I've dubbed it "the catacomb." It's a place that reinforces the fact that you are, officially, caged. When the prison was first built, there was a computer glitch and the locks wouldn't open. Panic and some others were trapped for over three hours. He said it was worse than a week of solitary.

Chapter 5

My grandfather's farrier was named Dale Barnett. He was a jovial, stocky countryman with a handshake like a vise and a filterless Camel cigarette dangling from his mouth, even when leaning over hammering on a hoof between his legs. As kids, Gil and I learned a great deal about horses by listening to him. We would sit around bombarding him with questions while our dogs got territorial over the hoof clippings. I think my grandad also enjoyed hearing Dale's stories about riding horses out west on the open range with one of his farrier buddies. He had been to Colorado, Wyoming, and Montana, places that Grandad never got around to visiting in retirement.

On one of his shoeing visits to the farm, Dale brought along his nephew Marvin, who, like Gil, was twelve. Marvin was built low to the ground and powerful. Marvin didn't play football, he told us, because he was too busy working on his family's farm. He would've been a great offensive guard. Thirty pounds lighter than Marvin yet fast, Gil was the starting running back on the seventh-grade team. Four years, two months, and twenty-three days younger than Gil, I was so skinny I looked like I had rickets. My third-grade biceps were the size of Marvin's wrists, maybe.

Grandad needed to talk to Dale and told us to go play.

"Behave, Marv," Dale said.

We started walking toward the bass pond. Gran came out on the porch and yelled, "Gilbert, you and Jack be careful now." This was family code for making sure that guests could safely ride horses or swim before we engaged in such activities.

"We've got a rope swing at the pond. Wanna do that?" Gil asked.

"Yeah."

"Can you swim?"

"Sure. You think I'm an idiot or something?" Marvin said.

"I didn't say that," Gil laughed. "I was just making sure. Your uncle's a friend of ours and we don't want anything bad to happen."

"Uncle Dale's a prick," Marvin said.

This language was a little shocking to me, in part because it was so unexpected. I glanced over at Gil, who shrugged his shoulders and kept walking.

"Why do you say that?" Gil asked.

"None your business."

"Why say it then? Why call your uncle that if you're not going to back it up with something? I like him."

"You would."

"You don't know anything about me," Gil told him.

"I know your name is *Gilbert. Gil-bert,*" he said, taunting and laughing. Gil's face was expressionless.

"You're right. That was my great-grandfather's name."

I decided not to say a word and just follow Gil's lead, a cautious enough approach at the time but one that unfortunately turned out to be a template for my adult life.

We walked past a vine-choked, rusting Allis-Chalmers tractor. I picked a chokeberry and squeezed it to see the purple stain on my fingers. I watched a wren flit in and out of a cedar tree, constructing a nest. I have thought about the events of this day for many years now. When I was a defense attorney, I became proficient at mitigation arguments. As the preachers all know, there is usually something good that can be said about even the worst of people, and short of that, at least some explanation (Prosecutors call it "an excuse.") that can be offered for a transgression. It is possible that Marvin's aggressive personality was the result of an abusive home life or a horse kick at an early age. Rationalizations are as endless as a lawyer's imagination.

At the pond, we started skipping stones. Gil walked a good distance away from Marvin. I remember thinking that Marvin knew enough about skipping to choose small, flat rocks, but he wasn't any good at it because of his throwing motion. Skipping stones takes finesse. It's not about brute force.

"Watch this, sports fans!" Marvin said as he picked up a larger rock and hurled it into the middle of the pond in the general vicinity of where some Canada geese were congregated. Gil was busy perfecting his skip technique and didn't see this. Marvin began walking quickly along the bank toward the geese, a good distance away from Gil. I followed him.

"And here's the pitch!" Marvin picked up a rock the size of a softball and threw it at the geese. This one landed within ten yards. The geese quickly dispersed.

It was over. He didn't hit one of the geese, thankfully. I blurted out, "That was *stupid*." Marvin squinted at me as if noticing my existence for the first time.

"Look who's calling somebody stupid." He put his right hand on my chest and pushed me down to the ground. As I was getting up, I saw Gil running toward us. Marvin pushed me again with both hands on my shoulders, forcing me into the pond. The mud at the bottom was like quicksand and I was up to my knees in it. I tried to wade back to the bank but it was slow going with the slimy suction. I heard Gil's feet pounding the ground as he ran past me. His right arm, cocked behind his shoulder, unloaded into Marvin's face. They both fell to the ground. Marvin's bloodied face looked as if Gil had smashed a ripe tomato into it.

Gil got up first and stood over Marvin yelling, "*Who do you think you are?*" Gil's right hand, still balled into a fist, dripped blood. His face was crimson. I had no idea what Gil or Marvin might do next. Adrenaline surging through me, I grabbed a wooden paddle lying beside the edge of the pond with the intention of hitting Marvin, if I ever got out. Marvin came to his knees, holding his nose with both hands. Then he began to sob; his heavy, choked cries sounded like someone hyperventilating. Gil backed away from him a few feet, but kept his fist up.

Marvin stood up and, out of breath, said, "I'm tellin'…Uncle Dale." He ran toward the house, taking quick strides for such a big boy. And then Gil did something that, in retrospect, defined his personality for me. He juked like he was going to run after Marvin, a quick step with his left leg followed by a convincing head fake. It was completely gratuitous, done just to amuse me, or maybe himself.

My sense of relief at the end of the altercation was accompanied by a metallic taste in my mouth and an upset stomach. I put the paddle down as Gil extended his bloodied right hand to help me out of the pond. He grimaced when I grabbed it. We learned days later that it was broken. Feeling queasy, I went over and sat down on an upturned canoe, then started puking. "Get it all out," Gil said as he washed his hand off in the pond.

We went straight to the rope swing. After all, it had been our initial destination. Within minutes, we heard a vehicle hightailing it out of the driveway, dust rising above the tree line. "Hospital," Gil explained. And just then the flock of geese returned, skidding along the lake in tandem, sending ripples toward us. I counted fourteen geese. Then my cousin yelled, "Watch this, sports fans!" and executed a flawless back flip off the swing. Seemingly suspended in midair, he laughed before falling toward the surface of the water.

§

Thinking about the farm so much led to the dream I had last night: As I was walking in a field, I noticed strands of horse hair, snagged on a barbed wire fence, blowing in the wind. I reached with both hands to loosen the hair and suddenly the fence wrapped around my wrists like a snake, slashing my veins. Blood pooled in my cupped hands.

What to make of this? How much time should I spend trying to interpret my dreams given that I have nothing but time? Are they better left unexamined?

Chapter 6

There was a fight in the control room today. This is unusual only because we haven't had a real one in almost three weeks, which must be some kind of record. Shoving matches, backhands, or bitch slaps that aren't retaliated against don't count around here. In fact, the guards don't even write these up as infractions anymore. Troll once told me: "If I did paperwork on every little scuffle in this fuckin' place, I wouldn't have time to hassle you losers." Understandable. Today's fight, however, requires documentation.

A new inmate, a young white guy, got into it with Torch, of all people, contesting the pecking order in our Unit. Torch is in his mid-thirties now, so he was spotting the kid a decade. I happened to be walking by and caught the action already in progress. People who've never witnessed violence firsthand have no idea how quickly it happens. Worried about the consequences, especially considering that Torch is my main protector, I immediately began to sweat. But it is impossible not to watch.

Both of them were handcuffed, but not to their waist chains. Even though you're joined at the wrist, both arms working in concert still make for a formidable weapon. The guy was about six foot with the broad shoulders of a laborer, but he was overmatched by Torch, who's 6' 4" and chiseled. The guy took a wild swing that missed by a foot and put him off-balance. Torch hit him hard in the throat with a jab, stunning him, and then landed a roundhouse square on the cheekbone, the sound similar to a baseball bat shattering. With practiced efficiency, Torch then elbowed him in the mouth, his neck snapping back like a crash test dummy's. He staggered backwards against the wall. Groggy, he appeared to be gathering strength to come back for more when Troll finally ran up and tasered him, perhaps saving his life. The guy seemed to cave from within, like an imploding building. There was a certain inevitability to it.

Then he bounced onto the floor and twitched for a good fifteen seconds before going limp.

The few onlookers, mostly black, rushed to congratulate Torch on his victory, their joy mixed with a sense of relief. Voices got much louder. Torch, out of breath and sweating, wasn't tasered because he didn't start the fight and was only protecting himself. Plus, loyalty is important here. The guards genuinely like Torch and also feel very fortunate that he's the top dog in the Unit because he has no interest in challenging their authority. He has accepted his status and has no plans to start an uprising or to attempt an escape. All he and his buddy Lars want to do is lift weights, to sculpt their pectoral muscles and abs. Since Lars is white and the only person capable of challenging Torch, their friendship is good for overall race relations. It is also a godsend to the guards, who are more than happy to let the Firm sort out matters of jail hierarchy, spreading peace through strength.

Curious about the aftermath, I leaned down and surveyed the new guy's face. It looked off-kilter, like a Picasso done in blood. On his neck, among several other tattoos, I noticed an Aryan Fist, the unmistakable mark of the Skinheads. I was then nudged out of the way by two guards who took off the taser probes and started shoving the guy's arms into a straitjacket.

"As soon as he's out of the infirmary, that motherfucker's *going* to the hole," Troll yelled. He put the taser down and began to fan his arms out as if breaststroking. "Everybody back up so we can get this piece of shit outta here. Earl, put on your goddamn gloves."

Blood was oozing from the guy's cheek, which had obviously been sliced by Torch's cuffs, and from his mouth, where the elbow had landed. I scanned the floor but didn't see any teeth. Beef arrived with a gurney. It took three guards to lift him. They tightened the straitjacket and the straps across his legs. He was barefooted, having come out of both sandals. The boy was moaning and cussing. As the gurney was rolled away, the wheels tracked blood across the white floor of the control room and down the hall leading to the infirmary, the trail fading from crimson to pink.

"Hey! Hey!" Troll shouted until Beef turned around. "Leave that jacket on him in the hole 'til I say so." Beef nodded.

Troll turned to me and said, "What happened? You see anything?"

"I missed the start. Did you see that Skins tattoo?"

"Goddamn Nazis. That fucker's only been here three days and thinks he's a badass. I shoulda let Torch go for a while."

I've fostered a relationship with Troll (real name Jerry Ferguson) for some time now. He trusted me enough to ask for a lawyer referral when his nephew got drug charges in my county, which made me feel good since I'm still a little sensitive about my disbarment, even if it was for a murder conviction. My guy kept his nephew out of jail and Troll has been appreciative ever since. Born and raised in a small community near Columbia, Troll is white, conservative, Christian, Republican, anti-abortion, and pro-gun yet also a harsh critic of any kind of white supremacist group, whether Klan, Neo-Nazi, or Skinhead.

His view is pragmatic: These instigators are hellbent on starting a race war in his workplace, which just so happens to be two-thirds black. He knows it won't be good for his job security if a war breaks out and the blacks end up killing all of the whites on *his* watch, especially in the great state of South Carolina. The prospect of losing his job would be enough to keep a guy like Troll up at night. Or, as he once told me: "Those white trash fuckers better be careful what they wish for. It might damn well come true and they ain't got the numbers. Most of 'em are chickenshit anyway."

I followed Troll as he walked over to talk to Torch. One of Torch's black buddies, Big C, whistled as if a good-looking girl was walking by. "Didya see my man Troll get the dust off that taser! Looked like John Fuckin' Wayne! Yeahhh, baby. *That's* what I'm talkin' about!" he said, yanking on his crotch.

An old, gray-haired lifer named Booker said, "Torch, this guard done saved your ass! You was goin' fuckin' *down*. Ain't that right, Counselor?" Booker likes me because I know a lot about his hero Miles Davis. We turn each other onto music and make fun of the crap that most of the inmates listen to.

"No question," I said. "That Skin had Torch on the ropes."

"He a Skin, for real?" Torch asked.

"Maybe," Troll said. "Counselor saw some ink that made him think so. You all right, big guy? You hurt at all?" Troll examined Torch's hands and elbows as carefully as a cornerman.

"Nah. I'm good."

"You look clean. Not a scratch. So what happened?" Troll asked.

"My boy beat the *shit* outta Adolf is what happened," Big C said, still celebrating. Troll fought back a smile.

"Be fair, now," Booker said. "Looked like dude was makin' a comeback when Troll used *excessive force* on the poor boy." In 1968, at the age of 19, Booker was sentenced to serve the rest of his natural life. To hear him tell it, he "got caught on the wrong side of a love triangle." Sounds familiar. A trusty here and at other prisons for over twenty years, he has a chess match with Troll every Wednesday and regularly beats him, "Just not your day, Jerry," his post-game gibe. He's completely self-educated. The guards let him be in charge of a clean-up crew and also run errands for them, so he has by far the broadest access of any inmate.

Booker is one of Miguel's favorites, despite Booker's use of colorful language. Miguel describes him as "very spiritual in his own way." Many times their sessions run long and I have to knock on the door to remind them that time is up. Seems I'm not the only prisoner who makes Miguel laugh.

"All right...all right. Let me talk to Champ," Troll said. "Booker, did you lose your mop or what? Look at this fucking mess." He motioned to the bloody floor. He looked at Big C and pointed up, a cue to get back to the business of replacing light bulbs.

As Booker walked off toward the utility closet, he started complaining about the task: "Can't you get some Klan fucker to lick this shit up. Ain't supposed to be *no* damn fights in the control room."

"Well, this is your area, ain't it? You're always braggin' about how spotless you keep it," Troll said, smiling at me and Torch.

From down the hallway, Booker yelled "If I get AIDS from some goddamn Skin's blood, there's gonna be a helluva lawsuit. My granddaughter'll be the richest woman in Charleston. Tell him, Counselor."

"Don't wear your gloves and you'll end up rich!" Troll yelled back. Then to us: "He'll never shut up about this. You know that." It occurred to me that, a generation ago, Troll might well have been a Yellow Dog Democrat. But all that's changed.

"Torch, did you ever have words with that boy before today? Any kinda run-in?" Troll asked, taking out his pen and pocket pad to take notes.

"Don't know him, I swear. Somebody say he new."

"So tell me what happened."

"Come at me from behind. Outta nowhere. Saw him just when Big C hollered at me."

"Hold on," Troll stopped him. "C, don't go anywhere. I'll need a statement from you too."

"Where would I go, Jerry?" Big C said, standing on a ladder.

"Yeah, yeah. Go ahead, Torch."

"After I heard C yell, I saw that boy jumpin' up at me. Going for the choke with his cuffs. But I got ahold his arm 'fore he got round my head. I threw him on the floor, but he come back up swingin'. That's when it went down."

It was a smart play by the Skin. A cuff choke is one of the few ways you can take out a superior opponent. Done right, you can crush his windpipe.

"How many blows, you figure?" Troll asked.

"Couldn't tell ya. When the shit hits, I go someplace else," Torch said, pointing to his temple.

"Just two and an elbow. Then you came," I said.

"I saw that elbow. *Nasty,*" Big C said.

"That Skin was dumb before, but his IQ just dropped twenty points," Troll said.

"You'll tell me when he gets outta the hole, right?" Torch said.

"You know we will," Troll said.

"How long can you keep him there?" I asked.

"I'm not sure. I'll have to talk to Hawk."

"What's the possibility of getting him transferred?" I asked.

"Probably slim to none. Who would want him?" Troll said.

Booker returned with a cup of water for Torch. He still didn't have the mop out yet. His adulation reminded me of Howard Cosell hero-worshipping Ali after a heavyweight bout. Torch drained the cup and handed it back to Booker with a subtle nod of appreciation.

When I got back to my cell, I was still amped up from the fight. I hastily wrote down some bullet points:

- Booker's right: Should <u>never</u> have been a fight in control room. Skin supposed to be waist-cuffed with no way to choke, b/c only been here 3 days. Protocol <u>not</u> followed.
- <u>The day Skin arrived</u>, Hawk a/o Troll should've reviewed file, seen tattoo listings and warned others. Guards have <u>got</u> to do <u>better</u> job. Prison grossly understaffed. Responsibility starts at the top.
- Now total of 7 Nazis, 2 in hole. How many unknown? Make sure Torch aware of them <u>by sight</u>. They stick together at Table 8 for Wed. dinner. Play ping pong on Sat. night at 6. Write warden letter about transfers/safety concerns.
- Think what Torch feels like <u>every day</u> knowing he's now a target.

I didn't sleep well. I got up at 4:30 and wrote more:

◆   Let the racists have their own little ethnostate somewhere in upper N. Dakota. Pathetic, brainwashed bastards. Living in a world without Miles, Coltrane, or Monk. No Sam Cooke, Marvin Gaye, or Al Green. No Four Tops, Jr. Walker & The All-Stars, The Spinners, Chuck B., Otis, Ray, B.B., J.B., Muddy, Buddy, Ronnie, Stevie, Aretha, Gladys, Curtis, Hendrix, Sly, Marley, P-Funk. <u>My man John Lee Hooker</u>. Those stupid Skins don't know what they're missing.

Lesson #2: You'd better get your allegiances straight before the day the shit hits.

Chapter 7

I am serious about peeling back the layers.

A conventional retelling is the only reliable way to do this; otherwise, I might end up playing fast and loose with the facts.

At the age of fifteen, I lied to my grandmother and told her I wanted to become a poet. Not that she believed me. This was at a time when Gil was racking up accomplishments in college: editor of the aptly named newspaper *Vanderbilt Hustler* in just his sophomore year; debate team; soccer team; and frequent contributor of short stories to the literary journal *Scrivener*. Somehow he found enough hours in the day to belong to a social fraternity and to date an array of stunning girls.

It was typical of me as a teenager to think in grandiose terms. Looking back, I don't recall ever feeling discouraged in the least when my dreams turned out to be short-lived. A year before, I'd told my dad that I hoped to be an NFL wide receiver, and just three months prior, I had informed Gil that I was going to be the new drummer for the Rolling Stones. Somehow, I would replace the masterful Charlie Watts after I arranged a private audition with Mick and Keith. Of course I did not have a drum set at the time.

I had shown no particular interest in creative writing, especially something as complex and demanding as poetry. In fact, my lack of engagement with literary matters had been a source of great disappointment to my grandmother, who was a retired high-school English teacher and a published poet of some note in our small community. Gran loved Keats, Dickinson, and Shakespeare (though, like Dr. Johnson, she didn't care for the Bard's puns). Many of the books in her expansive library contain copious notes in the margins. She composed mostly in couplets, sometimes alternate rhyme, and published in local periodicals, although two of her best poems made it into the *Sewanee Review*, securing her reputation as a serious artist. A devout Presbyterian and child of the Depression, she humbly referred to her poetry as "just a Sunday afternoon pastime."

Gran read to me often as a child—*Treasure Island*, Dickens, Twain, and the Bible (emphasis on the Gospels so as not to scare me away from it)—but what I remember most is her soothing voice in my ear and her fondness for smelling my hair as I sat on her lap. When I was about thirteen and she realized that I was in thrall to rock music, she attempted to "salvage what was left" of my intellect by giving me the *Collected Poems* of Dylan Thomas as a birthday present. In the table of contents, she had put check marks beside certain poems: "The force that through the green fuse drives the flower," "Fern Hill," and several others.

I read the checked ones as quickly and incuriously as I would a review of a film I had no intention of seeing. I had hoped for something to rival the intense exhilaration I felt listening to the Stones. Thoughtlessly, I never mentioned anything to Gran about the poetry, good or bad, after she gave me the book. I'm sure she had written me off as a lost cause.

So a few years later, my bringing up poetry came as a surprise to her. It was a rainy Sunday afternoon and we sat in her library, just the two of us. She was wearing her signature shoes. Crafted from a mold of her gnarled feet and specially designed for comfort by a podiatrist in Atlanta, they were something of a precursor to Birkenstocks. She knew that they weren't stylish and joked about them, but it didn't prevent her from owning multiple colors and wearing them on any occasion, casual or formal. I always felt like her unfashionable footwear lent more weight to her intellectual gravitas. Gran was somehow above silly trends and all the other ills she perceived as causing our cultural decline. Her shoes were one of the first things that former students remembered about her.

"Gilbert wrote me a beautiful letter," Gran said. "He seems to love Nashville. Have you talked to him?"

"Yes ma'am. I finally got him on the phone last week. He's not coming home again until spring break."

"Well, that'll be nice. Maybe you two can ride horses." Suddenly, she dropped her voice an octave. "And you, Jack, what are *your* plans for the future?"

Completely unprepared, I was like the guy who forgot the test was that day. To my own astonishment, I said, "I wanna be the new Robert Frost." I had glanced down and seen a book of his on the coffee table and remembered studying him in school. If pressed, I could not have told her the name of any of his poems other than "The Road Not Taken." Gran gazed at me with a bemused look I had not seen before. "Do you now," she said. She paused to sip her sherry, which she perhaps relied on too much in later life. "Well, poetry requires a lot of discipline," Gran said, caressing her sherry glass. "I didn't think you cared a *thing* about literature. All you talk about is sports and that awful music."

I could not meet her stare. I looked at the logs burning in the fireplace, listening to their soft crackle.

"I'm ready to get serious now," I said.

"Are you tired of being the class clown? I thought you enjoyed making people laugh."

"I do but..."

There was a long silence. Gran kept it like an oven in there because she was very cold-natured. I slowly pulled off my sweater and took several sips of my sweating Coke. Finally, blessedly, she let me off the hook. "Anytime someone puts pen to paper, it's a good thing, Jackie. I would love to read some of your poetry when you're ready to share it with me."

Yet I never did. Gran died unexpectedly that spring, in her garden where she'd been happiest, among the zinnias and sunflowers. She was 81. Gil had to come home before his spring break. It was the only time I ever saw him cry.

I didn't get around to writing anything that I, a tenth-grader, thought was good enough to show her. For many years, I felt guilty about not having produced a proper poem for my grandmother in her lifetime, the memory of this serving as a valuable lesson regarding my work ethic.

Gran's death affected every family member. Within months of her funeral, my once happy, confident, affectionate mother became sad and withdrawn. Back then, it was called a "nervous breakdown"; today it would be immediately diagnosed as a "depressive disorder."

I have distinct memories of when she stopped hugging me and how confusing that was for a teenage boy. Sometimes Mom wouldn't come out of her bedroom for days. When she did show up for meals, she was usually distracted and listless. She disengaged from everyone—my dad, my sister, grandad, Gil's family, her friends. She suddenly dropped out of clubs and groups and committees that had been the staples of her social life for decades.

And then she stopped playing the piano. This seemed unthinkable since she was classically trained and regularly performed at local concerts. She also taught lessons in our home from the time I was a little boy. Like Gran, Mom had enjoyed teaching and felt enormous satisfaction when students showed progress, but as she got sicker, my dad had to call the disappointed parents of her pupils and return their money.

There was no way to keep her depression a private matter in a small town like Warrington. People began being overly nice to me. The opportunity to leave town for a college two hours away was a welcome relief.

When I was growing up, my mother didn't believe a child should be awakened by the shrill sound of an alarm clock. Most mornings, she would open the doors between her music room and my bedroom and begin to play a Beethoven sonata or a Chopin nocturne on her Steinway. I would get out of bed and walk groggily to sit beside our dogs, who were lounging on the floor in a semicircle around the piano. When a ritual of that many years ends abruptly, you feel that you are somehow to blame.

In his matter-of-fact way, Dad told me that playing piano reminded my mom of Gran too much, that it made her think about performing for her as a young girl. My mother never said this to me, though. Instead, she insisted that she was merely taking a "a temporary hiatus" from the piano, but my dad and I were skeptical of this because she'd quit listening to music altogether. Her beloved records remained untouched in a tall stack by the den stereo.

It was difficult for me to tell the difference between the symptoms of my mother's depression and the effects of the various medications that her doctor had prescribed. During the spring of 1976, Dr. Harold Jenkins became a fixture in our household. An old family friend and a member of Dad's regular golfing foursome, he was a general practitioner who, by his own admission, had no expertise in psychiatric matters. After six months of writing prescriptions for various drugs and seeing no improvement in Mom's condition, he referred her to a psychiatrist in Charlotte.

Years later, my sister Rachel told me that electroconvulsive therapy had been considered by my mother, but the Charlotte psychiatrist decided against it. The procedure had fallen out of favor by the seventies, even in the South, and there was a certain stigma attached to this rather crude attempt to rewire someone's brain circuitry. I still believe Rachel's version of events, for it shows how desperately my mother wanted to get well.

Though the word was never uttered, the specter of suicide loomed over our house. I had questions that I never asked: How much worse will Mom get? Are the medications even helping? Will things get better? I found two books in the school library that dealt with suicide. When I checked them out, I told the librarian that "it's for a paper I'm writing." She nodded her head sympathetically. The books just made me more fearful.

It was a time of sudden transitions. Mom moved into my sister's old bedroom, supposedly because she'd become nocturnal and slept throughout much of the day. Since it wasn't fair for Gil's mom, Aunt Betsy, to bring us food all the time, a lady from our church offered to cook three days a week, and she turned out to be a genius with fried chicken. I was briefly heartened to see that Mom still had her sense of humor when she told me and Dad, "You boys sure came out ahead in the food department." But a few days later, when I happened to be looking out my bedroom window, I saw Dad take our hunting rifles out of the house and give them to my grandad for safekeeping. I learned not to get my hopes up too much and that every day probably would be different than the day before. A chemical imbalance was ruining every fucking thing.

My easygoing father's dark-brown hair turned completely gray in six months. Stress was not something he was accustomed to. Never one to worry about work, he dabbled indifferently in real estate and local politics, sometimes landing a lobbying position in the state capital. Prior to Mom's illness, he was so carefree that I thought the only thing he took seriously was his golf handicap. But once things got bad, it was like he found his true calling, becoming Mom's vigilant nurse, always on call, always there for her. To the outside world, he attempted to maintain his normal nonchalance, aided by a winning smile, but his gray hair told the real story.

My grandfather was so affected by his daughter's illness that he suddenly grew impatient with horses and began concentrating on the vegetable garden instead. I once heard him tell my dad, in what sounded like a pep talk, "I know these are trying times, Allen. I trust you'll let me know when you need some help, son." It was the only time I recall him referring to his son-in-law that way. They were an odd pairing, those two—the reserved, Depression-era Presbyterian always striving for the dollar and the gregarious, cocksure World War II vet who was careless with his money. One a Nixon man, the other a JFK fan, they had nevertheless always gotten along. Mom's problems brought them even closer.

I'm sure Dad leaned on him, having lost his own father at a very young age to polio.

To help out, Gil's dad, Uncle Robert, gave me a summer job as an intern at his law firm, xeroxing copies and delivering legal documents to the courthouse for filing. I now realize that Dad and Robert had cooked up a way to get me out of the house. Plus, I think Dad wanted me to grow up with a better work ethic than he had. At the time, I didn't know it would lead to a fascination with the law, much less a career. I also couldn't foresee that I would one day become Robert's law partner and he would eventually supplant Gil as my most trusted confidante. If Gil was jealous of my relationship with his father, he never said so.

Gil had a summer job with a publisher in Nashville but because of Mom he came home a lot more than he would have otherwise. With the best of intentions, Gil tried to stop being his normal wisecracking self and become the serious, consoling older cousin.

"I appreciate the gesture," I said. "I know you don't know what to say. I just want you to be yourself. *That's* what I need right now."

"Got it, Junior. So why don't you talk and I'll listen. That way I can't do anything wrong." He smiled and crossed his leg continental-style, an affected mannerism he'd picked up at school. We had always shared the truth about everything. I told him I wanted to know exactly what his parents had said about Mom's condition. His response seemed forthright. I had heard most of his information already, except for the fact that Gran had struggled with depression. This was news. I'd just assumed that poets were moody. I guess families have to hide things from children for their own good. Well, I thought, at least I have a culprit: the family DNA.

Gil said that his mother couldn't bring herself to talk about her sister's situation, and so he had to rely on periodic reports from his dad.

"It's that twin thing," Gil said. "You know how they are. All I know is she prays a lot for your momma."

Gil's comment barely registered. I was already a nonbeliever before Mom got sick. A born skeptic, I guess, tailor-made for the legal profession. Mom's illness just reinforced what I already felt, that Christianity was mythology, and I found Edith Hamilton's book on Greek and Roman myths more engaging than the Bible.

I'd grown up being a crucifer and an acolyte in the Episcopal church, mindful of its powerful symbology. I enjoyed the pageantry of the service and equated it with acting in a theatrical production, but I never bought in to the basic message. Nonetheless, I was very intrigued by those intelligent adults I knew who seemed to be devout. I figured out later that some of them were simply hoping nothing bad would happen to their families, and that organized religion was a more dignified, ceremonial way of rubbing a lucky rabbit's foot.

To take my mind off Mom, I immersed myself in rock 'n' roll. I was intent on learning everything I could about rock music, and it was an endless means of escapism. I became a vinyl shopaholic at the local record store, devouring lyric sheets and liner notes. I savored record reviews by my favorite writers at *Rolling Stone*. Granted, in a house of silence, my kick-ass stereo was somewhat wasted. When my mom did leave the house, usually to go to the doctor, I would blast it, neighbors be damned.

My tastes were diverse, egalitarian. I'd give anything a shot. I developed serious fixations with bands as different as the Clash and Grateful Dead, and with singers as distinct as Neil Young and Ronnie Spector. My desert island choices were cemented early on: *Let It Bleed, Eat A Peach, Born To Run, Kind of Blue*, and *What's Going On*.

I began to realize that it would be impossible for me to both listen to all of the essential albums *and* read the entire Southern canon as Gil had. So I took the easy route and chose the music, reading only those books assigned in my English lit. classes. Gil, however, read everything, including the near-unreadable such as *Absalom, Absalom!* And this was where our inner lives diverged, although being an intellectual didn't seem to make him happy.

One day Gil complimented the size of my LP collection and began casually thumbing through it. Starved for his approval since he'd once sung in a rock band, albeit briefly, I was ecstatic when he muttered "impressive, nice, excellent choice, love it." He started asking questions: "Do you like this album? Who's playing lead on that? Do you think she's a good songwriter? Do you like his voice? Do you think this is as good as the first album?" He actually wanted my opinion. Gil's recognition of my musical knowledge gave me a much-needed sense of identity. I would be the music connoisseur, an authority to be consulted even if I couldn't play an instrument. I realized that, if I continued on this path, music would be the *one* thing that I'd know more about than Gil. It presented a way to finally get out from underneath his shadow.

When Gil came to visit Mom, I normally let him see her alone while I stayed in my room. He was one of her favorites, charming her as he did everyone else. Still, much of his flattery of Mom was genuine, for he saw her as an artistic role model. He really did appreciate her talent and respect her work ethic, once saying, "If I spent as much time writing as you do practicing piano, I could win the Pulitzer."

Out of deference to Mom, and perhaps mindful of my feelings, Gil has never written about a depressed female in his fiction; there's no character that you could say was even loosely based on my mother. However, he may have written an entire book on my family and be waiting to publish it when I die.

I vividly remember one particular day when Gil visited, spending an unusually long time in Mom's room. I took off my headphones at some point. Dad joined them and they all started whispering, so I gave up trying to hear them. When Gil finally came back to my room, I casually asked, "How'd it go in there?"

"She's going to be *fine*." It felt like the first time he'd ever lied to me.

"Define *fine*," I said.

"She's going to get better. I think she'll come around soon. I really do, Jackson."

"Like she used to be?"

"Sure. This thing is only temporary."

Then Dad walked in without knocking. He was drinking a bourbon and water.

"You boys keep on talking, don't mind me. I'm just nosing around."

Neither Gil nor I felt like pretending that we were talking about anything other than Mom, so we remained silent and watched Dad. He stared at my posters of rock stars on the wall without making his customary jokes about their long hair and mine. He went over to the desk and thumbed through my homework, the first time I ever recall him doing so. Dad slowly took a drink, then looked directly at Gil and me. "You two are in a foxhole together. So look out for each other." And then he left the room.

I later learned that some family members were surprised that Mom hadn't taken her own life. She died of a heart attack, although her depression never eased. James Anderson, a former student of Mom's, played Debussy's *Reverie* at her funeral. When James came back to Warrington to visit his family, he started placing sheet music at Mom's graveside. Some of her local students took his cue and began to do the same. On windy days, as I passed by the cemetery on my way to court, I would sometimes see the music scattering across Eternal Gardens, floating onto graves, drifting through other people's lives. Whenever I could spare the time, I would gather it all up and put it back with Mom, under the heaviest rock I could find.

Years before she passed, my mom chose a few lines of Gran's poetry to adorn her gravestone. Interestingly, they didn't have anything to do with music, though many of those were available from my grandmother's collected works. Referencing instead the beauty and promise of springtime, Gran's words are hopeful, optimistic. I won't cheapen her verse by including it in the journal of a murderer.

Chapter 8

Today marks the second anniversary of my conviction.

Both prisoners and guards alike are affected by current events. Several recent prison escapes in Ohio, Kentucky, and Texas have made the national news. When hearing of these, most of my fellow inmates have cheered maniacally like British soccer hooligans. Jailbreaks give them hope, however unrealistic, and hope is the most precious commodity in here. I've heard them talking about it nonstop, especially Panic. He relishes the thought of "sticking it to the Man" almost as much as he does the idea of his own freedom. When the inmates in Kentucky were captured days later, hiding in the woods only a few miles from their prison, Panic was distraught, angry, and incredulous. He kept saying, "They couldn't steal a getaway car? How fuckin' hard is *that*? My ass woulda been in Mexico by now."

All of these escapes have been from older prisons with crumbling infrastructure. According to the news, the inmates in Ohio, who had some working knowledge of HVAC, discovered a compromised grate and were able to shimmy through the ventilation chases to the outside. Unfortunately, a new, underground facility like Congaree presents unique challenges. But the guys in here are much more knowledgeable than me about construction matters, and I won't be surprised if one day somebody figures out a way to get up to ground level. So then what? Unless he has a catapult ready and waiting, he will still have to deal with the sharpshooters in the towers and somehow scale a thirty-foot-high concrete wall topped with razor wire so sharp that it occasionally slices careless birds in two. If by chance an inmate should make it all the way to the yard, I doubt he'd fare any better than those poor birds.

Regulation 206 states that inmates, while on the yard, "must not communicate in any way whatsoever with the guards in the towers." It's commonly known as the "distraction rule." Like many regulations, 206 has at times been bent, depending upon the personalities involved. On the yard, I've heard Master chatting with one of the sharpshooters nicknamed Blink. They have a mutual friend. They used to shoot the shit about NASCAR mostly, then last week I overheard Blink tell Master they couldn't talk anymore.

"They're clamping down on us."

"Why's that?"

"Not sure. Had a big meeting with the top brass and they laid down the law."

"Earnhardt's still a pussy."

"You are what ya eat," Blink said, walking to the other side of the tower with an AR-15 resting atop his shoulder. The rifle cast a long shadow across the guard tower, making it look like there was a bayonet attached.

Panic went over to Master and said, "What's the deal with your sweetheart?"

"They say he's a crack shot. All that matters."

"Why don't he join the damn Army then?" Panic said.

"Wanted to. Got a bad foot."

"Sounds like a fuckin' Earnhardt fan," Panic said.

I can't help but wonder if the crackdown is a result of those jail breaks getting a lot of press. It could have come down from on high at the Department of Corrections, or it simply could've been a matter of our warden seeing his fellow prison officials in Texas interviewed on NBC and realizing that an escape would signal the end of his political ambitions. Losing an inmate would be great ammunition for an opponent during a debate.

§

Today on the yard, looking over the razor wire at the tall pines in the distance, I saw the two egrets circling. I've noticed them for the last few weeks. The birds seem to return to a location about a half mile away. I estimate that's where it starts to get swampy in Congaree National Park, a forty-square-mile hardwood forest bordering the prison. It's very much like the woods I grew up playing in, and this wilderness has taken on a mythical quality for me. If I could just get there and make it to the river, it would be impossible for the dogs to track me over water. Maybe I could have someone (who?) leave me a kayak and plenty of food and water. Enough to survive for a couple of days. There's a scenario in my mind where all of the pieces fall into place.

Before prison, I didn't know what true longing was. I thought I did, but it was just some romanticized bullshit. Longing, I now know, is not Jay Gatsby staring at the green light on Daisy's dock. Not by a long shot. That's *desire*, a completely different thing. Longing is being aware that what one desires is unobtainable.

§

In 2007, statewide remedial measures became necessary after two inmates in different prisons were killed execution-style for the same reason. Now, for their own safety, Congaree's pedophile child killers are housed separately in a special area which Ed has dubbed Diddleville. It's in a former psych ward located somewhere between Units 4 and 5. Currently, there are three pariahs occupying this space. These men interact only with one another and the guards. They don't ever eat with us and they're never allowed in the rec room at the same time as the general population. When outdoors, they're always at the other end of the complex, cordoned off by three separate chain link fences with razor wire. Despite these obstacles, Skunk's obsession is to murder these men slowly and sadistically. He has spoken at length about how he would do this. I'm tired of hearing it.

This afternoon, from some seventy yards away, we can see one of them walking around. It's the tall, lanky guy in his fifties with a high forehead. Skunk despises him most of all. He abducted a ten-year-old boy from a Winn-Dixie, molested him multiple times over several days, suffocated him with a plastic grocery bag, and then went to see a Disney film. Beef says that the other peds don't even like being around this guy.

Skunk walks over to me to bum a smoke and says, "I swear to God, I'm gonna filet that freak."

About a year ago Skunk asked me confidentially if I thought he would get the death penalty if he iced a diddler.

"Absolutely," I said, not wanting to encourage him. I didn't need anything else on my conscience.

Skunk asks, "How come *that* fucker ain't on death row?"

"Usually happens when the relatives of the victim don't believe in the death penalty."

"Screw that. I believe in it."

"Or the jury won't render a verdict of death because of doubts, for whatever reasons."

"Like Susan Smith's case."

"That's right."

"Another fuckin' child killer. I hear that cunt's got her a new husband, after she got caught screwin' them guards. They say it's some disbarred lawyer that married her. That ain't you, is it?" He elbows me in the ribs and smiles.

"No, not my type."

"Good. I'd hate to have to carve you up." He laughs and bums another smoke from me.

State prison is its own ecosystem. Through media and gossip, inmates keep track of the latest news about the most infamous prisoners in the same way free citizens digest *People* magazine to stay abreast of the lives of movie stars. Even though there are currently several serial killers in our penal system, including two remarkably sadistic psychopaths who've garnered national press, Susan Smith remains the most notorious inmate by far, and the most reviled. The brothers haven't forgotten that she lied and said a black man kidnapped her two boys. The nation believed her, until she cracked. Every inmate I've spoken with believes it was solely her fault for having sex with the two prison guards, that she, in fact, was the one who had all the power in the situation. They don't necessarily feel sorry for the guards; they merely think those guys were stupid and weak the way most men are.

"Dumb dicks seduced by the Devil herself," Skunk says.

Chapter 9

I had seen him several times before I ever talked to him or sought his wise counsel. He would be walking down the east corridor on a Sunday afternoon, en route to his visitations, talking with an accompanying guard. I was either sweeping the floor or taking a break. Once you see Miguel, you don't forget him. He has a bushy, unruly gray beard that takes up most of his sun-weathered face. Unlike most preachers, he is always dressed casually, given to wearing bright-white tennis shoes, ill-fitting "high water" Wrangler jeans that expose his ankles, and either some guayabera shirt or a Houston Astros baseball jersey with Escovedo sewn on the back. By contrast, the Episcopal reverend who sporadically visits wears a Brooks Brothers suit.

Miguel, bow-legged as a bronco buster, has the effortless swagger of a former athlete and a demeanor that connotes a seriousness of purpose. For a man in his seventies, his arms are surprisingly muscular, yet he always says, "I'd rather garden than go to a gym any day." He has a bulbous, broken nose (from street fights as a kid growing up in the slums of Mexico City, I later learned), rotten teeth that he's ashamed of, and some paunch spilling over his belt buckle. To me, the look in his brown eyes is both compassionate and hopeful, but I cannot be objective. At first, I assumed he was a maintenance man before I heard he was a chaplain. When I saw him here on Christmas Day, I wondered who would leave his family at such a time to go visit murderers in Hell.

I went to Miguel out of abject desperation. I knew I was starting to enter the Void, due in large part to a lack of exposure to the elemental: sun, rain, wind, clouds, rocks, trees, rivers. And women, certainly. For a while, I thought I might stop eating and drinking, not as a means of heroic protest, but rather out of surrender. But I knew I lacked the courage, for I feared oblivion above all else.

Still, in prison you vacillate. After being incarcerated for a year, I came to suspect that I might disintegrate if I didn't seek help. I questioned if a soul was, in fact, what distinguished me from the cockroaches also occupying my cell. Either way, I needed to talk to someone about the static in my brain, the chasm in my heart. That someone became Miguel.

When I signed up on Miguel's inmate list, mine was the only non-Hispanic name. We met the following Sunday in the same conference room where you go to see your lawyer, which is adjacent to the control room. Visiting the clergy necessitates one of the most thorough frisks that you undergo in prison. I brought along my trial transcript and the guard checked it carefully to see if I had hidden a shiv between the pages. The beige cinderblock conference room resembles a morgue. Miguel sat at one end of a metal table and I at the other, some eight feet apart. My right hand was cuffed to a steel eye bolt protruding from the wall. Per procedure, the guard left a door ajar so Miguel could easily escape to the control room if there was a problem. I put my trial transcript on the desk. Miguel was reading my file, which was spotless. Regulation 117(c) allows the chaplains, for their own security purposes, to have access to general biographical information (place of birth, age, family, etc.); specifics of inmates' crimes (methodology, weapons used, trial or plea, sentence); and their prison record (episodes of violence, disciplinary history), basically everything except medical/psychological information protected under HIPAA.

Miguel said, "I believe they call you Counselor. Is that right?" He had only a slight accent and his voice was much deeper than I'd anticipated for such a small man.

"On good days," I said, grinning. Miguel smiled back knowingly.

"Everyone calls me 'Padre' even though I am not one. It's easier than Escovedo." His melodious baritone would have been appealing to a jury.

I had thought a good bit about what I might say to him in our first meeting. Originally, I'd intended to let Miguel know, with appropriate humor, what an unlikely penitent he had before him. Ever since I was very young, I've thought that all religions are, in the words of Clive James, "advertising agencies for a product that doesn't exist." My position was only reinforced while practicing law. I'd seen too much bad in this world to believe that good predominates. Prime example: A child porn case that I was appointed on just two years into my career. I could hardly bear to review the discovery materials, most of which were videos found at my client's home. He kept these tapes on the bookshelves in his den beside the encyclopedias. His victim was an eight-year-old girl. If there were a God, he wouldn't let that kind of shit go on.

I thought about mentioning some other objections to faith and the Church, but I had plenty of time to discuss such matters. I opted to go at things another way. I didn't want to waste our first meeting, so I asked Miguel right out of the gate why *he* believes in God.

He calmly said, "Because my mother told me to and I obeyed. And that is how I was able to survive my childhood and help save my mother when she needed me most. At this point, my faith is habit."

He loved his mother. This was my guy. Thereafter, I found myself repeatedly apologizing for being so presumptuous and putting him on the spot. It was then that I first noticed him fighting back laughter and covering up his mouth with his hand. The teeth that I could see were brown-black and crooked. I felt bad that he was ashamed.

I told him that I was accustomed to people seeking my help and that it felt awkward to be on the other end of things. At the time of my disbarment, I explained, I had handled some 4,500 cases to their conclusion. That was a lot of people to talk to, he agreed. Consequently, I asked Miguel if he wouldn't mind telling me about himself first, before I did the same.

"As a boy in Mexico City," he said, "I had to scavenge food from street vendors to keep from starving. Sometimes I was so hungry that my stomach cramps made me cry. But I never cried in front of my mother. On Saturdays, me and my older brother, Luis, would go to the large street market downtown. We'd find a place on the other side of a hedge where vendors threw over their rotten fruits and vegetables. We figured out which ones were the pickiest about their produce and got behind them. There was competition everywhere from other kids who were just as hungry as us. The unofficial rule was that there was no fighting: The food belonged to whoever got to it first. You had to have quick reflexes and be very fast. It was a thick hedge and there was no way to know when something good would come flying over it. It was like they were throwing money in the streets." He said this as if it was his fondest child-hood memory.

I found out later that Miguel was in this predicament because his father, a postal worker, had been killed in a traffic accident when Miguel was only two. His Catholic mother had no money and no job skills other than domestic work. After an appropriate period of mourning, she took a boyfriend named Javier from a very prosperous family. He turned out to be a violent alcoholic who verbally and physically abused her. To escape the situation at home, Miguel would play soccer in the streets with his friends until dark. He became proficient at the game, quick with his feet. One day when he was eleven, Miguel came home to find Javier beating his mother with a soup ladle in the kitchen. There was blood on her face. His brother Luis was not there to help. Miguel did what came naturally and kicked Javier in the crotch several times, subduing him long enough for his mother to crawl to safety. Javier grabbed him by the hair and began hitting him with the ladle, but Miguel was able to get a knife from the kitchen drawer and slice his bicep. As he told this story, Miguel simulated the stabbing motion. Javier retreated to the bathroom and locked the door, allowing their escape.

Miguel, his mother, and Luis sought sanctuary at the Church of the Virgin of Guadalupe where a Father Arturo and several nuns helped them. The next day, wearing a bandage on his arm, a sober Javier showed up at the front of the church crying and begging Miguel's mother for forgiveness. Sitting beside her as she wept in the sacristy, Miguel could tell that his mother was moved by Javier's plea and that she was considering going back to him. This confounded Miguel. He could not understand how she could feel any affection for a man who had struck her child in anger. It was inconceivable that his mom would let him back into their lives and allow this ordeal to continue. "At that moment, I hated my mother," Miguel said. "I knew then that I needed to talk to Father Arturo about these troubling thoughts. He was the only adult male who had ever shown me any kindness. I had no memory of my own father, you see. Father Arturo was my hero, the role model I needed. A lot of the kids in my neighborhood felt the same way. He had been a well-known soccer player in his youth and he would play with us until his knee started hurting. He is the reason I wanted to enter the priesthood."

"If you don't mind my asking," I said, "what did Father Arturo say to you about your mother?"

"He bent down on one knee so we were eye to eye. He told me that my mother loved me more than life itself and to never question this fact. He said I needed to do everything in my power to protect her from being hurt again.

"In his wisdom, Father Arturo knew that, even if my mother moved all the way across town, Javier would track her down wherever she went. Two days later, Arturo called our family into his office and told us his plan. He said, 'Rosa, your boys need to hear this, to know what is happening. They are young men now who must listen very carefully to my instructions so they can help you on this journey.' He told me and Luis what to say if certain situations came up, assuring us it was 'okay to lie just this once.' Before this, the thought of going to America was like going to the moon. The chances were the same. It took money and contacts, two things my mother did not have. I didn't even know we had relatives living in Houston.

"It took a few more days for Arturo to work everything out and we continued to live in the church. I ate every meal with the nuns, who teased me about my cowlicks. One night Javier showed up very drunk and hostile. Father Arturo had to get the police to remove him. No charges were brought. I now see that Arturo did not want to get lawyers involved." Miguel looked at me and raised his eyebrows.

He continued: "I remember Arturo handing envelopes full of cash to my mother and to a white man named Turner who spoke only English. Early the next morning before dawn, Turner drove a station wagon to the back of the church by the playground and we got in. My mother thanked Father Arturo and hugged him goodbye, causing a look of great embarrassment on his face. She was a very beautiful woman, you see.

"Turner drove us north for two days. He didn't stop to sleep. Behind a Texaco gas station, we met up with an eighteen-wheel truck that took us and about twenty other people across the border. The trailer did not have good ventilation and everyone was very uncomfortable. My mother looked scared and sad. Somewhere in the Texas desert, we pulled over and all of us had to cram into one motel room and be very quiet until our contacts arrived to pick us up. Turner brought us pizza and water. He had been following the tractor trailer in his station wagon. After about thirty-six hours, my mother's cousin picked us up.

"Our cousin had been Americanized by marriage and thought he was better than us. I'll never forget he told me and Luis that we stunk. Even though he did us a great favor, I never saw him again." He shrugged his shoulders.

His dream of becoming a priest ended at age seventeen when he fell in love with Anna, a waitress at the restaurant where he worked as a dishwasher. After marrying her, he followed Anna's family to South Carolina where he and his mother found good seasonal work picking peaches and strawberries. (His brother Luis remained in Houston, also because of a girl who would become his wife). Miguel learned English quickly, if at times incorrectly or profanely, from his interaction with local farmers and co-workers. Eventually, he took over the business decisions for Anna's family, contracting with some thirty farms in both of the Carolinas. "We did the hard work that nobody else wants to do any-more," he said, scratching his bushy beard and laughing.

His mother, who never married again, worked until she was 80 and lived to be 87. In her later years she hated the taste of peaches. I asked Miguel to please bring me a picture of this amazing woman, and he said he would.

Miguel and Anna had three children, all of whom still live with-in an hour's drive of their father here in Columbia, much to his delight. He started his first church about ten years ago, shortly after Anna died from a long battle with breast cancer. "I needed to keep busy," he said. Though he had attended Mass at the same Catholic church for decades, Miguel wanted to have an informal, nondenominational outreach so that he could minister to as many working people as possible, acquaintances he had met through work "that seemed to be drifting spiritually, without purpose." He made it clear that he could not abandon Catholicism. I liked the fact that Miguel had no specific religious training or education-al degree, only a natural love of the Bible and its teachings.

His first Sunday *gathering*—he prefers not to use the word *ser-vice*—was held in the basement of a friend's shoe repair business and has since grown into a loyal congregation of some three hundred, about 50/50 Hispanic and white.

"The local VFW has been kind enough to rent me space for wor-ship, with the understanding that we need to be out of there before the first NFL game starts. They are a rowdy bunch!"

From Miguel's descriptions of the informality of the gatherings and the use of silent prayer/meditation, it sounded to me a bit like the Quaker experience.

I was surprised Miguel told me all this up front, but I was thank-ful he did. It was instructive. Based on my experience dealing with a vari-ety of people, I was certain that Miguel Angel Escovedo was the "genuine article," as Gran used to say. He was definitely not some con man for Christ.

When my turn to talk came, I remember thinking that, instead of having to sit in this sterile, depressing little room, I wished Miguel and I were in a boat on the pond at the farm, fishing for bass and drinking cold beer. I'm always running back there.

"This is the transcript of my trial," I said, turning to the page I had marked.

"I must tell you," Miguel said, "I do not know the laws."

"You're lucky. That means you haven't been in trouble."

"It is true I have not used a knife on anyone since I was very young."

"And it was justified from what you told me."

"These are things only God can decide."

"What I'm going to read you is not about the facts of my case. This comes after my cousin and I have already been found guilty and we're about to be sentenced. Members of the victim's family get to speak about the impact of the case on them and what kind of sentence they want."

"Yes, yes." He nodded. "I have been to court for people before. On both sides."

"This," I said, waving the transcript, "is one of the many reasons I'm here to see you."

As I scanned the page to find the passage, a vision of the young woman in the courtroom came vividly back to me. She was very tall in high heels and dressed like a corporate professional. Even though I was still reeling from the verdict, I do recall being intensely conflicted when she began to address the court. I still hated her father, but I simultaneously felt very sorry for her. Her whole body shook with anger. Despite my feelings, I read her words in my normal voice:

"These two men have destroyed the lives of everyone in our family. I've been a Christian woman my whole life, but I *cannot* find it in my heart to forgive them. On behalf of the Crowder family, we ask that you sentence them to life in prison and not a day less. They deserve the death penalty, to rot in Hell."

When I finished and looked up at him, Miguel avoided eye contact. It had gotten very warm in the conference room by then, my nasty orange shirt damp, clinging.

"Imagine someone saying that about you."

"May I call you Jack?" he asked. Something about hearing Miguel say my name made me start crying. Deep, guttural heaves, impossible to muffle. Judging from the look on his face, I don't think Miguel was expecting this from me any more than I was; after all, I'd come into our meeting with considerable bluster.

I asked him if he wouldn't mind closing the door that opened into the control room, and he kindly did so.

"Privacy is good," he said.

"Thanks. You can't let these men see..."

"I know," he interrupted.

Miguel took out a small plastic pouch of Kleenex from his pocket, walked across the room, and put it beside me on the table. Prepared, like a funeral director. He came within a foot of me, close enough that I could've grabbed him with my free hand. Yet Miguel never worried about his safety around me.

He gave me some time to regain my composure. I fully expected him to quote some scripture on the subject of forgiveness, perhaps a passage from Matthew. But he didn't. Nor did he ask me about my own religious beliefs. Instead, he said, "Jack, are you still helping prisoners with appeals?"

"Yes."

"Does this take a lot of your time?"

"No, I only have one right now and I'm almost through with it. What's on your mind?"

"I need some help. I'm looking for volunteers."

"I'm probably the wrong guy to spread the gospel."

"It's nothing to do with religion."

"What then?"

"A friend of mine started the prison literacy program. I thought, with your background, maybe you could help. Some men here read below fifth-grade level; some are illiterate. If a poor boy from Mexico City can learn English, anyone can, right? We want to give them opportunity and that takes good teachers."

"I'd like to think about it, if that's okay. I taught a law course once and didn't feel like I really had the patience you need to..."

"Yes, yes. You're doing us a favor to consider it. Thank you, Jack, yes."

Miguel easily led me down the path he'd laid out, as I had once led witnesses on cross-examination. He surmised that the best way to change my life's negative trajectory was to help others. Although I left our first meeting still a nonbeliever, I was a convert to the potential healing power of confession.

Chapter 10

I guess it's time to explain how I ended up in prison. I've put it off long enough. And yet, how do I make sense of chaos, and how can I give form to disorder?

I must be careful here. I'll need to guard against the temptation to get in a hurry. But isn't this a tendency we all have, to fast-forward through the bad shit?

At 4:35 p.m. on January 16, 2012, Gil and I sped through the front gate at the residence of Eric and Regina Crowder, thinking it would be closing at any moment. Traveling over sixty miles per hour, our Subaru began to fishtail in the first curve of the long driveway. Gil slammed on the brakes but, still going about twenty, we crashed into a large oak tree. The impact on the passenger side crushed my door, knocking me unconscious "for about thirty seconds," according to Gil's testimony. I came to with Gil shaking me and screaming, "Jack, he's got a gun!" Things were hazy, but one thing I did remember was that we weren't carrying one.

I was so scared that I tried to get out with my seat belt still on. Gil moved the airbag aside, unbuckled me, and helped me crawl over the driver's seat and out of the car. That's when I heard the first pistol shot. I couldn't tell what direction it was coming from. "Keep your head down!" Gil screamed. He grabbed my arm and pulled me directly behind the car. Fortunately, the hatchback still opened. "Hurry, help me find the tire iron," he said. A second shot hit the car and ricocheted. We ducked for cover.

"Hurry!"

"Where's he shooting from?"

Gil pointed directly over my right shoulder. I found the compartment, removed the cover, and handed him the tire iron. He whispered, "Stay down behind the car and *don't* move until I tell you. Understood?"

"Where are you going?"

Gil never answered. He crawled along the length of the driver's side, paused, came to his feet, and then ran off. I crawled where he'd been. Another shot echoed. I worried that Gil had been hit. I couldn't yell out because Eric would know I was still behind the car. I suddenly realized that the dying car's hissing and clicking would make it difficult to hear Eric if he was to sneak up on me. I quickly glanced around the front of the car and didn't see Eric or Gil. Crawling to the back, all I could see was the pickup truck we had been chasing just minutes before. Was Eric there? I heard nothing. My hands clenched the cold grass. Time slowed. I started to feel increasingly vulnerable behind the car. I knew I was going to die.

Then several shots were fired in rapid succession. Gil screamed, "Jack, come quick! Get his gun! Jack! Jack!"

I scrambled from behind the car and looked in the direction I thought Gil had yelled from. I didn't see anyone. Scanning the yard to my left, I saw Gil and Eric, both lying on the ground, face up, a few yards apart. I ran over to Eric, who was semiconscious and mumbling something. His eyes were closed and blood was draining from his right ear. I grabbed the .25 Beretta he still held loosely in his right hand. He didn't resist. I placed the barrel against Eric's heart and pulled the trigger several times, but the clip was spent. I tossed the gun down and grabbed the tire iron on the ground and hit him in the forehead as hard as I could. Once. Twice. Again. There was a cracking sound. He stopped moaning.

I ran to Gil, who'd been shot once in the right shoulder. His eyes were open and he was grimacing in pain. The bullet had hit the bone.

"It's over," I said. "He's dead." I took my shirt off and compressed his wound.

"Find Regina. I'll be fine."

I heard sirens off in the distance. That's when I realized that Eric must have called the cops during the chase. As a lawyer, I could already sense the wheels grinding.

"Help is on the way," I said. "Stay still. I'm sure she'll be down when she sees the flashing lights."

We had thought Regina was at home and in peril. Neither was true. She had gone to Florida, unexpectedly and hastily, to help a friend care for a sick horse. She hadn't gotten around to telling Gil; it's not like they were married. Her absence was just one of the many problems we later had at trial.

There was no getting around the fact that the owner of the property was dead in his front yard. Later, my attorney, Fred Mobley, a seasoned, cynical veteran of the courtroom, said, "At the very least, Jack, you should've moved his damn body out to the highway."

When four cops arrived, yelling with guns drawn, I raised my arms as high as I could. Eric's blood was splattered on my face, hand, and arm. I was grabbed by the back of the neck, forced to the ground face down, and handcuffed behind my back. I was thoroughly frisked. My wallet was removed. I had no cell phone, and neither did Gil.

Detective Dave Garrett said calmly, "What the fuck happened here?"

"It was self-defense. He was trying to kill us. He shot my cousin. We were trying to keep him from hurting his wife. You need to make sure she's okay in the house."

"You're not telling anybody what to do. Understand?" Then he immediately dispatched a deputy to check the house.

Another deputy who'd been looking over Eric came up to Garrett, handed him a driver's license, and said, "The bashed-in head is the homeowner, Eric Crowder."

"Nice place Mr. Crowder has here. Will he make it?" the detective said.

"Nah. Looking like a corpse."

When Regina was nowhere to be found in the house, I was placed under arrest for murder. Garrett said, "Your story isn't adding up, pal." To test for gunshot residue, he removed my cuffs, put evidence bags on both hands, flex-cuffed me over the bags, and reapplied the hand-cuffs.

Garrett put me in the back of his cruiser and buckled the seat belt, then left to process the scene. He instructed a young deputy to keep watch over me. Two medics carefully placed Gil onto a stretcher and then into the back of an ambulance. His hands were bagged for evidence as well. The flashing red lights illuminated my cousin's frightened face, the first time I'd ever seen such a look. I realized that Gil would have bled out if I had driven him to the ER. Eric's call had saved him.

A semicircle of cops and EMTs gathered around Eric. Some-body was already taking pictures of the crime scene, the camera's mo-mentary flash creating a macabre tableau. A deputy casually roped off Eric's cooling body.

When Garrett came back to the car, he turned on his video cam-era and read me my Miranda rights from a plastic card he kept in his wallet. I refused to give a statement until I spoke with a lawyer. Frus-trated by my decision, Garrett said, "Why? You *are* one." I had already formulated what our best defense would be, but I wanted a cooler head to concur with that decision. And I needed to talk to Gil, to make sure he hadn't concocted one of his elaborate fictions believing it would help us. Regardless, Garrett resented my pleading the Fifth. He thought an innocent man just wouldn't resort to that.

I was taken to a plain interrogation room where I sat alone for over two hours, handcuffed behind my back to a chair. The cops were waiting for forensics to arrive and take swabs of blood, blood I couldn't wipe off because of how I was cuffed.

Upon arriving, Forensics Sergeant Ned Wallace said, "Okaaayyy, Mr. Merritt, Esquire, in the spirit of 'do unto others as you'd have them do to you,' I'm gonna put this little mask over your mouth, just like I got on, so that the bubonic plague doesn't fuck up our night any more'n it al-ready has been. And I can tell you're not gonna give me one bit of trouble seein' as you're a cut above all those shifty fuckers you always represent, right?"

I wondered how many defendants had spit on him in his career. He put on plastic gloves, cut off my flex-cuffs, and carefully removed the bags from my hands. He painstakingly took twenty-four swabs, talking the whole time. He then removed my mask and photographed each place where he found blood. When taking facial shots, he continued to fuck with me. "Big smile," he said. He collected DNA samples from my mouth, then swabbed my hands with nitric acid so the crime lab could test for gunshot residue.

Two other officers came in, removed my handcuffs, and had me strip down to my underwear. Wallace put on a new pair of gloves, gathered my clothes, and placed them in evidence bags. The tan jumpsuit that I changed into smelled of cigarette smoke. It made me want one.

Afterward, they took me to a holding cell where I was finally able to wash my face and arms in the sink. No other prisoners were in the cells. I started to think about all of my prior cases that were like mine. There had been many over the years, with vastly different outcomes. Exhausted, I was about to doze off when they came to get me for fingerprints. The female officer who rolled me yawned several times during the procedure. She didn't apologize.

My one phone call was to Emily. A part of me wished that I could simply leave a voice mail. Without much time to talk, I had to get down to the business of instructions: Call my paralegal Gwen and tell her what happened. She'd make arrangements for a lawyer to be present at my bond hearing. Alert Gil's people in New York of his potential charge. Don't drive to the jail because they won't let you visit. Do not speak with anyone else about this matter—cops, the press, friends. Then I told her that I loved her. Throughout the call, Emily, crying, kept saying "No, Jack. No." It was both a desperate warding off and a heartbreaking plea.

I didn't get to shower until the next morning. It made me feel less dirty, but not cleansed. The cool water ran over me, pooling in a soapy, rust-colored film by the drain.

Later, an officer came to the cell and handed me a copy of my warrants. Garrett had filled out the affidavits. Concise like most warrants, the first one read:

> The defendant, Jackson Walker Merritt, did willfully and unlawfully violate S.C. Code of Laws 16-3-10 (Murder) in that he, with malice aforethought, did cause the death of the victim, Eric Boyce Crowder, by striking him in the head with a tire iron. This occurred within the county of Logan. The defendant declined to provide a statement.

The second warrant, for *Conspiracy to Commit Murder*, alleged that there was "an agreement" between me and Gil to engage in the act of murdering Eric.

Quite purposely, the cops put Gil in the cell facing mine. Once the reality of your mistake fully registers, you will do almost anything to escape the loneliness of a holding cell. Even talking to someone you hate at that moment seems better than thinking about your future. Gil and I had plenty of time to talk, but the subject that was most on our minds was one we couldn't raise with the guards within earshot: blame assignment.

He told me that he was formally charged the next day after he was transferred from the hospital to the jail. He'd arrived with his right arm in a sling, carrying two warrants with the same language as mine. His prescription dosage of hydrocodone was monitored strictly by the jail nurse. His repeated requests for more meds were consistently met with a firm refusal. "That bitch makes Nurse Ratched look like Florence Nightingale," he said.

Without my having to tell him, Gil knew that the guards and jailhouse informants would be listening to every word we said, so he didn't discuss the incident except to occasionally blurt out something generic and self-serving such as "How can they charge us when it was *self-defense?*" or "*He* was the guilty one." He spoke with the dramatic flourish of a lawyer in closing argument, but he appeared utterly devastated. I had seen this look many times before in the empty eyes of those suddenly facing murder charges. I didn't need a mirror to know what I looked like.

The headline of the *Warrington Chronicle*, "Local Lawyer Charged in Murder," was above our two color mugshots. Gil said, "See, you've got top billing. As it should be." Poorly written in haste, the article didn't even mention that we were related. I learned nothing useful from reading it, and I knew that any future journalism on the subject would be much more sensationalized.

I'm sure Gil and I both were experiencing PTSD. Violent death does that. I paced my cell while Gil snickered at the graffiti on the wall. He then bragged about the famous people he had profiled over the years.

I'd forgotten how many articles he'd done. He reminisced about writing a story on attorney F. Lee Bailey (pre-O.J. trial), a five-page quickie for some forgotten publication. Gil said he never met Bailey, whose schedule was too full, but he and a magazine photographer were allowed to take pictures of his palatial law office to include in the article. Bailey's secretary also provided them with a glossy photo of her boss, taken two decades earlier, for use in the piece. Finishing the story, he asked "Since you seem to be tied up right now, who's the *other* fucking F. Lee Bailey around here?"

On the second day, after appearing to take a nap, Gil suddenly stood up and stared at me through the cell bars as if he was imparting some urgent news. "You spend your whole life trying to write the book, then you realize your life *is* the book. Damn." Pretentious MFA stuff, I thought, and just nodded my head. I knew that anything I said would be wrong.

When the nurse came to change his bandage, Gil said he'd do it himself since she lacked "the gentleness required for this or any other intimate activity between a man and woman." She said fine. He didn't do a very good job with it, spilling hydrogen peroxide everywhere and struggling mightily to put the tape on using just his left hand. The nurse silently watched his efforts from the hallway, her arms crossed.

After three tense days, our bonds were set at one million each. Ultimately, we had to use the farm as collateral, something we didn't want to do. It was meant to keep us from fleeing to a non-extradition country. God, I wish I had.

Chapter 11

As so often happens with ping pong, Easy Ed got overly excited about the prospect of a rare overhead smash and hit the ball some two yards past the back edge of the table. It flew over to the chairs against the wall, ricocheted off a leg, and rolled two tables away. In a rare show of emotion, Ed threw his paddle down on the table. I made a mental note to hit more lobs in the future.

"Goddamnit! You're a lucky fuckin' lawyer." Ed groused. "I'm going to take a leak."

To retrieve the ball, I had to walk toward the table where Badger was playing. His sleeve tattoo is a comprehensive homage to hate: "Blood and Honour" across his bicep, a swastika, a Celtic Cross, several skulls, and a large 88 on his forearm. (H is the eighth letter of the alphabet; 88 stands for "Heil Hitler.") It's all there in bright red and stark black. I noticed he had a nasty abscess on his forearm, a wound he hadn't taken proper care of that had become badly infected. It was unpleasant just being near him.

My ball had come to rest right at his feet. He bent down and picked it up, then said, "Some day your big nigga ain't gonna be around to help you."

"What are you talking about?" I said, holding out my hand to receive the ball. I was trying to stall him while I quickly scanned the exact locations of Torch and the guards. Torch was only twenty yards away, but his back was turned and he couldn't see what was going on. Unfortunately, the nearest guard was young Ditto, who was reading the newspaper instead of monitoring inmates. As always, to call out for help would be cowardly, something you couldn't live down in a unit like ours.

Badger said, "We heard you was laughing it up with your boys when our friend Jason got attacked."

"You must have me confused with somebody else." I put my hand down, as he clearly had no intention of returning the ball. His playing partner, Drip, has a teardrop tattoo below his left eye. This facial ink has always struck me as superfluous. We know you killed someone, that's why you're here. Drip quickly walked over and backed me against the wall. Before I knew it, I was hemmed in pretty good. Lesson # 3: Don't get outnumbered.

Drip said, "Don't act like you don't *know*, fuckface. Y'all had a goddamn party after the fight." He moved even closer, a few feet from striking distance. They're both a little shorter than me, with less reach, but they're also twenty years younger. I widened my stance to prepare for whatever came next. I hate waiting to be hit.

Badger said, "Well the party's over now, asshole."

He crushed my ping pong ball in his hand and threw it at me. It bounced off my chest and landed on the floor.

"You have been pumping iron," I said as the puckered ball spun to a stop.

You can't back down from these fuckers and you can't let them see your fear, although mine was obvious in my voice. Still, I was in no mood to take any shit from racist scum at three o'clock on a Wednesday.

I finally made eye contact with Torch. He hurried toward me. Easy Ed, his bathroom break concluded, then slid in behind me by the wall.

"What's the problem here?" Ed said. "You punks don't have anything better to do than pick on my man here?"

"*Awww*, looka here," Drip said, "Ain't that sweet. All your butt buddies coming to help you out."

As Torch arrived and stood beside me, Badger said, "Here he is to the rescue! *Boy*, you gonna pay for what you done to Jason."

"We doin' it now?" Torch asked.

"No, you dumb fuck. There ain't gone be no warning when we come for your ass," Badger said.

Lars materialized out of nowhere and stood shoulder to shoulder with Torch, both members of the Firm now accounted for.

"You're a fuckin' disgrace to your own race," Drip said.

Lars, a man of few words, simply stared at Drip.

Emboldened, I just had to keep talking. "Hey, guys, it's really not their fault. I'm sure their parents are dumber than dogshit too. It just runs in the family." Easy Ed put his hand on my shoulder to calm me. He was right, as usual. I was going too far.

"It ain't always gonna be four against two, Counselor. You're good at law, we're better at math," Badger said, his eyes darting.

"You mean five against two," Panic said, suddenly appearing on the far side of the pool table. Drip turned his head and said, "Nobody counts a little wigger like you, Panic."

"You better, 'cause it ain't nothin' for me to whup a man's ass," Panic said. Lars chuckled. I was too scared to laugh.

Ditto finally arrived, waving his taser around.

"What took ya so fuckin' long," Panic said. "Been in the tanning bed?" It's obvious from his orange-tinted skin that Ditto does, in fact, make use of a tanning bed, more fodder for the inmate's ridicule.

Standing some twenty feet away from everyone, Ditto said,

"Who wants the taser today? Don't matter to me who gets it. Panic, you wanna stick out your tongue?" His radio then squawked. I thought I heard Hawk's voice.

"We're glad you're here, Deputy Fife," Badger said. "These shitheads came over and messed up our ping pong match trying to start something."

Drip said, "Ditto, why don't you start out by shockin' the monkey." He pointed at Torch.

Badger got a kick out of this and began drumming his paddles on the table. He sang the chorus of Peter Gabriel's song, butchering it badly. Second only to getting out of this prison, my greatest wish was that Torch would drive his fist through Badger's face.

Then Troll came running down the corridor followed by a stocky guard called Bravo who also had a taser. Troll was carrying a billy stick in one hand and his radio in the other.

Badger simulated a radio's squelch with puckered lips and said, "Sheriff Taylor's on the scene."

Troll yelled, "Everybody spread out in a wide circle where we can see you. Put your paddles down. *Now!* Don't think for a minute I won't send *everybody's* ass to the hole!" For the sake of appearances, he was being evenhanded.

"How can ya do that when we ain't been fighting?" Drip said.

"You *want* there to be a fight, smart guy?" Troll said. "I'm sure that can be arranged. Now what's going on?" He looked directly at Ditto, who said, "I just got here."

"Aren't you working the rec room? Never mind. Torch, talk to me."

"They talkin' big. Messing with Counselor," Torch said.

"Whatcha askin' that smelly ass nigga for? He the teacher's pet?" Badger asked.

Troll stared at Badger with a mixture of frustration and bewilderment, then said, "Son, if you've got that kinda death wish, why don't you go ahead and kill yourself. It would save me some paperwork."

Panic said, "Sarge, I think you oughta let 'em fight it out with a promise nobody goes to the hole for it! I'm taking bets. I say the Firm in less than thirty seconds."

"Enough, Panic," Troll said.

Drip said, "This here's *our* fuckin' ping pong table! Look where everybody ended up. They're on our property."

"What about it, Counselor?" Troll said.

"My ball rolled all the way over there. I went to get it. I should've..."

"Then what?" Troll said.

I was thinking about how careful to be in my description when

Easy Ed said, "They cornered him."

"You was in the can," Drip said. "You don't know shit, lyin' moth-erfucker."

Badger said, "He come over to our area and started talkin' shit, knowing the buck would back him up. That's the deal."

"No, the *deal* is rec time is over for every single one of you. Ev-erybody's getting put in waist chains and going back to their cell blocks," Troll said.

"Aw *fuck*! That don't include me, does it? I just came over to watch," Panic said.

"It includes you, especially your mouth," Troll said.

Panic said, "Well, I want Bravo cuffin' me. Ditto cuts off my cir-culation on purpose. I can't feel my damn hands for two hours after. I *got* civil rights!"

In the end, Badger and Drip went without a fight, which meant they didn't want to go to the hole on this day. But I knew that wouldn't always be the case. They were still talking shit to us as they were escorted down the east corridor. And they were planning.

Troll personally put leg chains on both of the Skins, but Bravo didn't use them on the rest of us. Troll instructed Ditto to handcuff Pan-ic and then immediately report back to the control room. He checked on their tightness. They were okay but Panic told Troll, "The boy's not *that* dumb. He ain't gonna do it with you standin' right there."

Troll said, "Why don't you quit giving him shit all the time? It *could* make your life easier. He's just twenty-three and in training. If you run him off, the next man up could be some veteran who gets his kicks crackin' your skull. How would you like that?"

"He's right, Panic," Lars said unexpectedly. "That boy was scared shitless today. If he knew you had his back, he mighta been quicker to help Counselor."

"So now *I'm* gettin' blamed?" Panic protested.

"That's not what we're sayin' and you know it," Easy Ed said.

"One day the Skins could come after you and Ditto might be the only one around to help. No Firm anywhere in sight. What you think's gonna happen then?"

"If they come for me, they better bring their *fuckin'* A game," Panic said. This made Torch laugh and Troll shake his head because Panic couldn't weigh more than 120 pounds. We all know Panic's story. His dad murdered his mom in front of him when he was seven. Shot her in the kitchen while she was doing the dishes. His father finally died last year at 82 in some penitentiary in Louisiana. Panic never had any contact with him. He talked to me about his dad once, saying, "I thought that motherfucker was too mean to die." I believe Panic has been searching his whole life for the Firm's kind of brotherhood.

When I got back to my cell, I wrote yet another letter to the warden, in lawyer's prose, expressing my "grave concerns" about the safety of this prison due to the rise of the white supremacist population, as well as the lack of adequate staffing. This is my eighth letter to him. He has never acknowledged receipt of any of them, not that he's under any legal obligation to do so. Regardless, it's infuriating. I'm still not accustomed to being ignored.

I am always careful not to criticize the job that Troll and the current guards are doing; I only stress the critical need for more good guards. In my letters, I have often sung the praises of Troll, Hawk, and Beef by name (their real ones). Troll says the warden has never mentioned any of my letters to him or to Hawk. When I ask if they've discussed the Skinhead issue, he usually says "Yes, the warden is aware of the problem."

"That's not the same as doing something about it, though," I once said in frustration.

"I understand. But the first questions are 'what' and 'how.' The 'when' comes last," Troll said.

"How about segregating them. Or do transfers to dilute large groups. Harsher discipline."

"He says D.O.C.'s working on it."

"You see anything changing?"

"Don't hold your breath, Jack. But keep writing letters."

So I do. I wonder if the warden even bothers to read them. Does he take me for a troublemaker? But why wouldn't he want to have a face-to-face with one of his more educated prisoners, to get an insider's view of what's really going on? Maybe he's passing all of my letters on to a superior within the Department of Corrections in an attempt to actually remedy the problems. Or does he think I'm planning on filing a lawsuit because I was once an attorney? I've tried to allay such fears in my letters, couching my comments as "merely suggestions on security measures."

My uncertainty is not surprising. Rarely seen, often talked about, and totally mysterious, Warden Herman Gulledge is nicknamed Oz. He addresses us publicly twice a year: once on Christmas Eve to profess his love of Jesus and once on the Fourth of July to proclaim his love of America. Other than that, he hides behind the thick curtain of correctional bureaucracy. I'll bet Booker knows more about what's going on in this prison day-to-day. You would think we'd see the guy walking around the halls of his own establishment more often, but maybe he, too, is scared shitless, like me and Ditto.

Oz is middle-aged, portly, balding, and prone to wearing cheap, ill-fitting suits, his coat sleeves often reaching to his knuckles if he's not bending his arms. I'm certain his experience with criminals at Congaree will serve him well should he make it to the statehouse.

As soon as I finished the letter to Oz, I wrote in my journal:

Questions:

*Why did I really go over to retrieve the ball by the Skins' table? There was a box containing some 50+ spare balls on the counter in the rec room. Is it really about fighting the good fight, or am I just trying to break the monotony? Or do I have a death wish? Or is my guilt such that I feel I deserve their abuse?

*Who is the gossip from the control room who ran his mouth about the fight? Inmate or guard? Unit 4 is a small town and word travels fast. Did they mean for it to start a shit storm? Innocent chitchat or bad intent? Maybe Ditto, not knowing any better, spoke out of school?

I went to bed late and had a shape-shifting dream. The first part was a memory: Emily and I were at a Peter Gabriel concert in Atlanta. There was throbbing music, bright strobe lights, a throng of fans. We had great seats, fifth row. When the band finished its encore, "In Your Eyes," the guitarist threw his pick into the audience. It landed at Emily's feet and I quickly scooped up the bright yellow souvenir for her. An unexpected birthday present. We kissed.

Then the dream immediately shifted to a fight between me and Badger. We were both wearing prison orange but the fight took place at the Peter Gabriel show. We were on the floor wrestling around among the concertgoers. The spotlights were on us, not the stage. It was an intense, life-and-death struggle. Emily screamed. The abscess on Badger's arm, filled with pus, was spotlit, making it seem grotesquely oversized. He began choking me, his right forearm, the one with the abscess, clamped across my throat. I struggled for air, began to panic. As I was running out of strength, I desperately kicked my legs around, trying to get some leverage. With one last burst of strength, I was able to move his arm off my throat and onto my face. I gasped for air, then Badger's abscess burst, spilling pus into my eyes.

I woke up retching.

Chapter 12

Bad dreams may sometimes be offset by happy memories. All you can hope for is to feel human for a little while.

I met Emily Graves in Charleston during the 1996 Spoleto Festival. This was back when I still envisioned myself as something of a ladies' man. I was avoiding the crowds in the Market and in Marion Square and decided to walk down a quiet cobblestone street where only a handful of artists had their paintings displayed. Beside St. Mary's Catholic Church, there was a young woman working intently at her easel, unconcerned about passersby. She wasn't looking up to talk in hopes of drawing attention. She didn't need to—she was wearing blue jean shorts and had long, gorgeous tanned legs. There were some older, married couples milling around, the men glancing without their wives noticing.

Her eight finished paintings, all unframed oils, were leaning against the wrought iron fence of the church playground. Each one had a sticky note attached, with the picture's title in quotations and a price below it, all handwritten in curlicued purple ink. They ranged in style from realistic landscapes (coastal marshlands, mainly) to fantastical abstracts. I thought they were good, certainly much better than the tedious pictures of Rainbow Row for sale on every street corner in Charleston.

While she worked, her shoulder-length brunette hair hid her face.

"You should charge more. These are excellent," I said, standing no more than three feet away, purposely crowding her.

"Thanks." She didn't look up. I noticed for the first time that she was left-handed.

"At these low prices, I guess I'll have to buy them all." As soon as I'd said it, I cringed.

"Hilarious," she said, deadpan. "Did Jill put you up to this?" She still didn't look up from her painting.

"I don't know Jill. I only know good art when I see it," I said, testing my limits.

She ran her non-painting hand through her thick hair, brushing it from her face, and then gazed straight at me. Immediately I knew she was too young, possibly still in college. But her green eyes were stunning, perfectly set in her face, like emeralds in a ring. She had, however, several neatly sewn stitches lined horizontally across the bridge of her patrician nose.

She yelled across the street to a young dreadlocked girl seated at a table selling jewelry. "*Jill!* Is this fella one of yours?" She pointed at me like I was a defendant.

Jill shook her head.

"Oh, I thought you were...She's been messing with me all day."

"I'll bet Jill's a real practical joker. How's she doing selling that jewelry?"

"A heckuva lot better than me!" she laughed. She had a cackle like Elizabeth Taylor. It was totally inelegant, almost preposterous. I immediately heard my future in it.

I leaned toward her as if to share a secret, then put my index finger on the bridge of my own nose.

"Are you a boxer as well as an artist?"

"Looks pretty bad, huh? Now see what you've done. You've made me feel self-conscious about it," she said, grabbing a pair of very large sunglasses and putting them midway down her nose.

"You look fine. I was just curious."

"Nosy might be the better word. Pun intended. Or maybe just rude," she said, turning away from me to watch two shirtless guys jogging by.

When she finally turned back around, I apologized. In my desperation, I found myself pointing across the way. "I'm like Jill. I like to kid around, that's all."

"*Lighten up!*" she said, laughing again. "Boy! You can dish it out but you sure can't take it, can you?" Smiling, she switched her paintbrush to her right hand and extended her left to me for a firm, vigorous shake.

"I'm Emily."

"Jack."

"And I couldn't care less what anybody thinks. About my nose or otherwise. Well, except my painting. I've got a lot of education invested in that."

Fifteen minutes later, I had a dinner date, or what I hoped was one. She was looking around in vain for a scrap of paper to write on so I gave her my business card. She glanced at it without comment, then on the back wrote down Palmetto Bistro 7:30. I felt like the jury was still out on whether or not she would actually show up. She may have just been trying to get rid of me. But, either way, I had insisted on buying a painting—a marsh with tiny seagulls in the distance. It hung near my desk until I no longer needed an office. She said she couldn't let me buy all of the paintings if she was going to dinner with me. "I know about you lawyers and your quid pro quo."

And her nose? It turned out that she'd been trying to put up a bookshelf in her apartment and thought it was secure until it came tumbling down on her head, cutting but not breaking her nose. The doctor said there could be a slight but permanent scar. "I'll be like a Cossack, I guess," she said. "They were very proud of their wounds, you know. They would show them off, bragging about who had the best scars. Totally macho."

"Like me."

She slowly looked me up and down, head to toe. I was wearing khaki shorts and Sperry Topsiders. I had joined a fraternity in college and my sartorial sense never quite recovered. Then she turned back to her easel and applied some cream-colored paint to a cloud she was working on.

"Don't be ridiculous," she said.

The twenty-six minute wait for her to arrive at the bistro was interminable. Emily's problem with punctuality never improved; her excuses for tardiness merely got more creative. I couldn't even enjoy the view of the Cooper River from my table on the patio. I watched a Navy submarine slide underneath the bridge. I fiddled with my napkin, debating whether to remove the silverware. Overhead, a squirrel scampered along a limb and then jumped to a power line that led him to the roof of the restaurant. At 7:45, I went ahead and ordered a Scotch. Despite a breeze coming off the water, it was still muggy. I thought about smoking a cigarette, but I resisted, not knowing if she might be offended. Emily's teeth were too white for her to be a smoker. The lack of nicotine made me edgy.

When she finally arrived, her hair was still wet. She wore a sundress and sandals and carried a brightly colored Peruvian shoulder bag that, I later learned, she'd gotten on a family vacation in Machu Picchu. I stood up and held out her chair, inadvertently cutting off the maitre d's attempt to do so. She slid in effortlessly.

"Thanks," she said. "Hope I'm still considered fashionably late. It took me forever to pack up all my stuff in this heat." She gulped her water. "I see you've already started."

"Yeah, the owner came over and said I couldn't just sit here all evening without getting something. They seem to be in business to turn a profit."

She threw her head back and got the waiter's immediate attention as only regulars can.

"Hey, Robbie. Vodka martini with an extra olive, please. How's your grandma doing?"

They chatted for a while about various family members and friends. Emily was looking up at him, which allowed me to stare at her without being rude. For the first time, I noticed a light-brown birthmark on her neck, just above the right collarbone. No more than an inch long and a quarter inch wide and resembling the outline of the state of Florida, I at first thought it a tattoo.

Once we ordered dinner, Emily and I settled into each other's company and began to share our respective bios. I've always been a good listener and she had a lot to say. She spoke quickly and authoritatively, telling me that she'd attended undergrad at Williams College in Massachusetts because it's a great art school and a long way from Charleston. "Unlike some of my friends, I knew there was life beyond the Holy City. It's like they were chained to a lamppost on Meeting Street, waiting for Rhett Butler to ride up and rescue them."

Emily loved Williams, but she had underestimated the frigid winters. She often would daydream about the stifling humidity in Charleston just to make herself feel better in January snowstorms. She made good grades, she explained, because it was easy to stay inside and read. "Plus," she added, "I didn't have the distraction of a steady boyfriend."

"That's encouraging."

"Not that I was looking for one."

Emily then spent a work-study year in Madrid and became "obsessed" with the work of Velázquez. Not surprisingly, she was at the Prado much of the time, staring at *Las Meniñas* and *Christ Crucified*. I could only hope that my occasional nods of the head would pass for some understanding of her intensity. I remember hoping that she wouldn't ask if I'd ever been to Spain.

When she returned from Madrid, Emily opted to get her master's degree in art history from the Rhode Island School of Design ("RISDy", she called it). "I know what you're thinking: cold weather *again*. But I already had all those sweaters! What was I going to do with them down here? Have you ever been to Providence?"

"Not yet, it's on the list. But remember, Emily, I'm usually working twelve hour days."

"Well, you *need* to. Go to Providence, I mean. It's very clean, not so much as a gum wrapper on the streets. You'd think you were in Austria or Switzerland. I hate trash and trashy people, don't you? There's no excuse for it. The other day I saw some guy driving down East Bay Street toss a bunch of beer cans out of his window. I caught up with him at the next stoplight and you better believe I read him the riot act. And do you know, that idiot had the gall to shoot me the bird."

"I'd be careful. People are crazy nowadays. I handled a road rage case once and..."

"Oh, you better know I had my mace, buster! That was one of the nice things about Providence. There were no rednecks. No one flying Confederate flags or spitting tobacco juice out of the windows of their pickups."

"So you've met my cousins."

"You're funny."

"I try."

The Civil War-era patio was uneven, the erupting roots of an oak tree having mounded the red bricks. Coming back from the bathroom, I tripped on a brick. I put my hand on a chair to steady myself. Emily, to her credit, did not laugh. Embarrassed, I blurted out, "Smooth move."

"You're blushing. I thought it was a nice recovery," she said. "I should've warned you about the bricks. My friends and I call this patio a field sobriety test."

"The sad part is I'm not even drunk."

"I'm not really in a position to be calling you a klutz," she said, pointing to her stitches.

As Emily's hair dried, it began to lift in the breeze, much like the Spanish moss hanging from the oak tree beside her. The occasional gusts exposed her simple, understated earrings made of broken glass. As she finished her first drink, I noticed that the tips of her fingers on her left hand were lightly stained with tints of blue and green. She caught me looking and quickly said, "Occupational hazard. I didn't have time to scrub it off. Think how ticked off you would've been if I was over thirty minutes late."

"I wasn't ticked," I said, perhaps too defensively.

"What would you call it? Miffed?"

"Anxious. I've never been stood up."

"If I say I'm going to do something, I do it, Merritt."
As the alcohol started to kick in, she continued calling me by my last name and her laugh rose to a soprano.

A natural cynic, I was caught off guard, astonished, actually, by my thoughts and feelings. Unlike the optimists and born-romantics I knew, I expected love to be elusive. I had never believed that life *owed* me a specific level of joy. From what I had observed thus far, the disappointment that accompanied most people's dashed expectations seemed to make them miserable, and occasionally inconsolable. When something good happened to me, I always figured it was best to be pleasantly surprised.

A strong wind came through and scattered all of the lightweight items on the patio. Bev naps flew toward the side wall as if drawn by a magnet. An elderly lady sitting beside us lost a hat that would've looked right at home at the Kentucky Derby. Emily laughed. The lady, looking perturbed, turned to us and said, "That hat catches the wind like a goddamned kite. What the hell was I thinking?" I retrieved the hat.

"That was sweet," Emily said.

"I would've done that even if you weren't here. Just so you know."

A light rain started, a precursor to the approaching downpour. Sheet lightning pulsed within a dark nimbus cloud. People hurriedly grabbed their plates and dashed indoors.

"So much for dining alfresco," Emily said. "Hurry. Follow me. Careful on the bricks!"

In the scramble, we got the last two seats at the bar. Syncopated rain pelted the windows. The lights in the bistro flickered, the patrons' gasps followed by nervous laughter.

"*Tourists*," Emily murmured. "But Spoleto is good for restaurants and artists."

"Did any of those tourists buy your paintings today?"

"Nah, but nobody ever said it would be easy." Emily peered into her martini, swirled her olive around, then ate it. "My mom was a portrait painter. And a good one. She warned me. There's a lot of competition out there. But I really, *really* don't want to lower my prices. That's the thing. I worked my ass off on every piece you saw displayed today."

Our waiter, Robbie, looking wet and harried, found us and asked if we wanted to hear about the desserts. We were both too full and I asked for the check.

"Remember, my offer to buy all of the paintings still stands. No strings attached," I said. There was no reaction to this, so I continued, "You said your mom *was* a painter. Is she not anymore?"

"No, she gave it up. The typical story. She was a perfectionist. It got to where painting no longer gave her any pleasure. Happens with most artists at some point. I get it. But for now I still love to paint. That's why I'm going to Paris."

"Vacation?"

"No, I'm hoping I can stay a year or more. I'll have to find some kind of employment. The folks at RISDy are putting out some feelers for me, but what they line up wouldn't be any great shakes. It would end up being what is affectionately known as *academic secretarial*. I can type and make coffee, but my French is more than a little rusty."

"I'd think that would be a deal breaker," I said hopefully.

"Not really. My friend Nadine made do and I'm better than she was. It's not like I'm going to be a translator. I bought some of those tapes but it's pretty boring learning that way."

"Do you know anyone living in Paris?" I asked.

"At the moment, not a soul. Nadine's job at the Sorbonne ended. I visited her twice when I was living in Madrid. That's when I knew I needed at least a year. Some things in life you should take your time absorbing."

"Sounds lonely not knowing anyone there. So when are you leaving?"

"After I save up a little money."

"I've been to Paris. You'd better save up more than a little."

A married couple, leaving with their young daughter, noticed Emily and came over to talk. I stood for introductions. They were the Pearces. Their little girl, Clara, was very cute, with blonde hair and big curious eyes. She and Emily had a mutual admiration society born of babysitting. "She lets Clara stay up past her bedtime," the father playfully admonished.

"Hop up," Emily said, patting her lap. As they talked, Emily constantly ran her fingers through the child's hair.

"Can I touch your stitches?" the child asked.

"Sure."

"No, Clara Louise," her mother said. "Don't be rude. Your fingers are dirty." The girl scrutinized the fingers of her right hand with a scrunched-up, investigative face.

Clara looked at me and said, "There's a boy named Jack at my school. I like that name."

"And I really like the name Clara."

The mother said, "Honey, we have to go. We don't want to intrude."

"Is he your boyfriend?" Clara asked, grinning.

"No, sweetie. We're just friends."

As they were leaving, Clara gave Emily an intense hug and waved goodbye theatrically as she exited.

"When you grow up here, Charleston is a small place," Emily said.

It was ten o'clock when we left the bistro. Outside, the night sky was clearing. Steam rose from the streets and sidewalks. Storm drains gurgled. We walked on East Bay toward Broad Street. An ATM illuminated some kids skateboarding in a bank parking lot.

We strolled past Chapter Two, the independent bookstore where, a decade earlier, Gil had a reading and signing for his first short-story collection. This was back when he genuinely thought he might become famous. It pains me now to admit it, but I told Emily about his reading there. I think I was feeling a little inferior in the wake of her worldly adventures and used Gil's accomplishments to impress her. She seemed interested although she'd never heard of Gil, a fact which would have distressed him to no end.

"He has a following," I said, "a small but loyal readership."

"Yeah, like me. My following consists of my family and close friends. Oh, and now you."

She peered into the window at the bestsellers on display. "Do you think I can buy your cousin's book in here?"

"It's probably not in stock. They'd have to order it. I warn you; his sentences can run a whole page. Gil prides himself on not having a plot. And he uses esoteric words that send you to the dictionary every few minutes. He's actually too smart for his own good. Shows off a bit too much. Quotes Joyce's *Ulysses* at parties."

"Well, he is kin to you," she said, pushing my arm, a mock-taunt. "I never could get through *Ulysses*. It just wasn't enjoyable. Reading started to feel like a chore."

"I prefer *Dubliners*, especially the closing story."

Emily reached into her Peruvian bag. She had more stuff in there than most people take on a two-week vacation. Eventually, she extracted a monthly planner and a pen.

"OK, *Dubliners*. And what's your cousin's last name?"

"Hampton. Gil Hampton. He inherited his talent from my grandmother, who wrote poetry in her spare time. She was published too. I wish she was still around. Now you talk about a great lady! In her seventies, she could quote Shakespearean soliloquies verbatim. She was one of those no-nonsense schoolteachers. I never could get anything over on her. Nobody could. You two would've hit it off famously."

Her planner in hand, Emily stood still as other pedestrians passed by us on the sidewalk. She stared at me with the intensity of a conscientious juror.

"You're full of surprises," she said.

"Gimme your address and I'll mail the poems. Is it that hard to believe there's intelligence in my bloodline?"

"Yeah, kinda," she said, laughing. Despite her fancy Northern education, Emily's speech had lapsed into a familiar Southern colloquial under the influence of alcohol. "If there's no such book by your cousin, you're cold-busted, Merritt."

"Where are we headed?"

"A little hole-in-the-wall bar. Wanna go or not?"

"Lead on," I said, sweeping my arm.

The moon was rising over the rooftops of Broad Street. For an instant, as we approached Saint Michael's, the harvest moon seemed balanced atop the church steeple.

"Hold on, Emily. Let me show you something." I gently turned her toward the church.

She stood silent. The only sounds were car tires slicing along wet pavement and rainwater dripping off copper eaves. The moon rose. We began walking.

Emily insisted on taking me to Demimonde, a basement rock club with a low, water-stained ceiling and cinderblock walls painted black and blue. It was packed. The bartenders were caged behind chicken wire and steel bars. Dungeon motif is OK if you're free to leave.

I felt old. Some goths with black fingernail polish gazed disapprovingly at my sport shirt. I took their disdain in stride though, confident in the knowledge that they would one day require the services of an attorney like me, if they hadn't already. The bartenders ignored me, so I had to get Emily to order drinks. The music was playing at brain-lesion level, everyone screaming to communicate.

Emily dragged me to the dance floor when she heard the Breeders' "Cannonball." It's a great rock song, but it's not the easiest tune to dance to. I like it best when driving on the open road with the windows down, on the way to the party—anticipation, then release.

Afterward, Emily gave me a hard time about staring too long at a buxom girl in a black leather bustier who was dancing beside us. Emily is small-breasted. This felt like an unfair test, but I did in fact fail it. Over a heavy bass line, I shouted, "You're a much better dancer than her, if it's any consolation."

Emily waved a dismissive hand at me. "It just goes to show the fundamental difference between men and women."

"Which is?"

"*Say that again?*" She cupped her ear, leaned closer.

"*What's the difference?*" I shouted louder.

She waited a moment, laughed, then yelled back at me: "*Women fake orgasms. Men fake relationships.*"

A guy standing near us turned his head in our direction. Given the lateness of the hour, he may very well have thought he'd heard something profound. I had never heard that one before and couldn't help but wonder how much of this hypothesis was based upon personal experience.

I waited a long time but the DJ didn't play anything that you could slow dance to. His fans preferred the frenetic. Would Emily have slow danced with me? I think about this more than I should these days. At my urging, we left the rock club to the hipsters.

Emily zigzagged through the city, taking shortcuts known only by locals. Familiar landmarks were darkened outlines. A girl wobbled her bicycle down the sidewalk, running us off the curb. Late-night drunks staggered side streets. Emily was lost in thought, but she looked at me every once in a while and smiled, which was enough. We ended up on King Street near the intersection with Broad, walking past Berlin's Clothiers where I would later purchase a burgundy and gold tie to wear at our rehearsal dinner party.

As we headed east on Broad, we heard a racket in Washington Square park: a continual yelling back and forth, angry and profane. Two twenty-somethings were five feet from each other, pointing fingers. A lanky preppy was defaming the mother of a short, stocky Citadel cadet, who threatened to "completely fuck up" the other guy's face. A sobbing young girl in a formal black evening dress stood to the side of the preppy. She was holding a pair of high-heeled shoes in her hand. Emily started heading in the girl's direction. I held loosely onto her arm, saying, "Trust me, you shouldn't get involved in that. Do you know them?"

"No."

"If you stick around here, you might go to jail. Explain that to RISDy."

"For *what?*"

"Whatever the cops feel like. Let's go. This is my area of expertise." With my hand a little firmer around her elbow, I guided her down the sidewalk past the park. There was no resistance.

"I'm coming," she said, so I removed my hand. "I want to know what I could be charged with for just being there."

"Public drunkenness, disorderly conduct, breach of peace. Want more?"

"But I'm not..."

"We're both drunk, Emily. And if we're around dumbasses who are being rowdy, we might get busted too, depending on the mood of the cops when they get there."

"I felt sorry for that poor girl. We should've at least brought her with us."

"No thanks. You don't know her. She's out with a knucklehead past her bedtime. She'll have to learn the hard way."

"Practicing law has made you a bit cynical."

"Not cynical...realistic."

About forty yards down the street, Emily stopped and turned around to look back at the argument, which still involved just a lot of pointing and screaming.

"Why do guys *do* that?" Emily said with distaste.

"There's not going to be a fight if that's what you're concerned about."

I explained to her that, in my experience, if those kids were really going to come to blows, they would've already done so. Now too much time had elapsed. They were simply posturing at this point. I also surmised that, if they were actually to fight, the military guy would stomp the preppy. And furthermore, I believed that the only reason he didn't was because his military punishment for doing so would far exceed any civilian consequences. He would be commanded to do a couple thousand push-ups in full dress uniform in the stifling heat. It simply wasn't worth it to him.

"Just a theory," I said.

She took a left onto Church Street, saying, "Almost there." We were near where I had shown her the moon over the steeple earlier in the evening. We had come full circle. There was no car traffic on the side road. We then took a left onto a quiet residential street. Other than our footsteps, the only sound was palmetto fronds swishing in the wind. We walked over the shadows of dogwood trees.

I said, "I wish..." She quickly pressed her index finger to her lips, shushing me. I drew closer to her and whispered, "I wish I could go hang out with you in Paris for a year, but some of us have to work."

"You're working pretty hard tonight. You understand there's not going to be any sex, right?"

"Never crossed my mind."

She stopped to look at a yard on a corner lot. She brushed her hand across the wet blossoms of an azalea bush by the sidewalk. "You should see the garden hidden on the other side of that wall. I swear Mrs. Rutledge has the most gorgeous little fountain in the city. She got it from some village in Italy. She's eighty-four now and I absolutely love her. She works in that garden every day. Gets more done than people half her age. And she wears the most stylish gloves you've ever seen."

"I'd like to meet her some day," I said. "You're going to miss her when you go to France."

"For sure. But I'm not going forever."

She casually extracted a ladybug from her hair, then carefully placed it on a hosta plant. I noticed the moon's reflection in rainwater caught in the curve of a leaf. Tonight, the mysteries of the universe were tuned to my frequency.

Emily began walking toward the end of the street. It turned out that she was living in an upstairs carriage apartment attached to a large Georgian-style Single. The home belonged to the best friends of her parents. This arrangement, I felt, allowed her to save face by not having to live at home at age twenty-five. The whole setup seemed very Charlestonian to me: claustral, protective. Sharp as she was, she probably had no idea how privileged her life had been. Underneath that no-nonsense, wise-cracking exterior, I sensed vulnerability. She certainly hadn't been exposed to life's harder edges. I seriously doubted that she could make ends meet in Paris on academic secretarial work. One way or another, I figured she would be on daddy's dime.

As we got to her driveway, she stopped and said, "Be very quiet, Jack. She's a light sleeper. And watch out; the fourth one up is a burglar step. I know that, historically, you have a problem with tripping."

"Only when I'm sober."

The wooden steps creaked beneath our feet. At the door, I could tell that she was nervous for the first time all night. She started fidgeting with the house key, turning it round and round in her hand. She unlocked the door. Then she turned, placed both hands flat against my chest, stood on her tiptoes, and kissed my forehead once, lightly.

"Thanks for a wonderful evening, Jack," she whispered, not making eye contact. "You *really* shouldn't have. Please be careful going down the steps." Then she walked inside, closing the door behind her.

Chapter 13

It all started with a friendly request from Miguel. He asked me "to look out for" Brian McLauren, a new inmate called Thin Lizzie, one of Easy Ed's most creative nicknames. Miguel had met with him only once but knew immediately that there was something different about him. Despite the horrendous nature of Lizzie's crime, Miguel believed that he was genuinely searching for some type of salvation in here. I'd seen the guy from afar and had no idea what he was like.

Lizzie mutilated his wife's lover with an axe, the extreme number of "whacks" drawing comparisons to the infamous Lizzie Borden. Pure jealous rage. I've handled similar cases and I can tell you this: The methodology suggests more about Lizzie's love for his wife than it does his hatred of her lover. Lizzie is 6'4" and no more than 160 pounds. The nickname, Ed said, was meant to be.

Lizzie mainly keeps to himself, a thirty year old with the maturity of a teenager. I've watched him closely for the last few days. At first I thought he was merely bashful and didn't like to make eye contact, but then I realized that all of his social interactions with the men seemed awkward. One day I watched him obsessively arranging the items on his food tray, lining up his milk carton perfectly parallel to his plate and plastic knife. When I've spoken to him, Lizzie exhibits a noticeable "lack of affect." He says the most mundane of sentences repeatedly, like a mantra.

For their part, his fellow inmates have variously described him as "weird" (Skunk), "fucked up" (Panic), and "a basket case" (Master). Booker simply said, "The boy ain't right." I've told the men he can't help it and that they should just ignore him. And for the most part, they have. The term I'd use to describe him is *fragile*, which I'm well aware sounds inconsistent with the circumstances of his crime.

A few days ago, a guard gave me a peek at Lizzie's file and I learned that he's actually well beyond a basket case. I can't say I was surprised, but I'm certainly alarmed, for him more than anyone. The forensic evaluation revealed that he suffers from a "Major Depressive Disorder" (Axis l) and a "Personality Disorder with Avoidant and Schizotypal Traits" (Axis ll). He "overcompensates for his intense feelings of inadequacy with grandiose fantasies." Socially inhibited, he suffers from paranoia, poor concentration, and anhedonia (the inability to experience joy). He receives Prozac for his depression as well as an antipsychotic. Despite this fact, the forensic psychiatrist at the department of mental health didn't believe Lizzie's diagnoses rose to the level of a psychotic disorder, which by statute meant "that he was aware of his actions on the date of his offense and was thus able to distinguish legal and moral right from wrong." He had no criminal record prior to the incident. That was all I had time to read, but it was enough to let me know how he avoided the death penalty.

The upshot is that Lizzie, despite his faulty wiring, is not ill enough to take advantage of a defense of *not guilty by reason of insanity*. Nonetheless, if Lizzie's attorney had been remotely competent, he could have negotiated a plea of *guilty but mentally ill*, which would have at least kept his client out of the general population where he doesn't belong and instead placed him in a more suitable psychiatric care facility within the Department of Corrections.

In the toxic environment of Unit 4, Lizzie's inability to interpret the simplest of social situations could cause tragic consequences for him and others. What if, for example, Panic wanted to have some good-natured fun one day and decided to rearrange Lizzie's little Zen garden on his dinner tray? It's possible that his reaction to Panic's joke could be inappropriately violent, even for a prison. You simply don't know. Prison life is unpredictable enough without adding Lizzie to the mix.

After scoping Lizzie out, I talked to Hawk about him. I spoke casually, careful not to mention anything that I'd gleaned from Lizzie's medical file.

"I don't know if you've noticed. That guy Lizzie has no business being in here."

"You think he should be in the loony bin?"

"I do."

"Booker said the same thing. What are y'all up to?"

"Booker who?" I said, smiling.

"I hear ya. I haven't spent much time with him yet."

"It'll be obvious, I think. Something's not right."

"What do you think it is?"

"Not sure. Did they do a psych?"

"Can't say. You know that. I'm not in charge of placing 'em. We've had a lot of messed up folks in here before. This ain't the glee club, you know."

"Just trying to make your life easier."

"And it's appreciated. But transfers take time. We've been over this."

"Is it *that* hard to get someone reclassified to the mental ward?"

"Usually, best I recall. It's been awhile since we did it."

"Speaking of transfers..." I nodded toward the west corridor where some of the Skins were walking toward the dining hall. "Wouldn't it be nice?"

"Don't push your luck with those boys, Jack. I don't want you gettin' in a bad situation again."

"I'm staying clear, don't you worry. No more ping pong when they're around."

"The axe man you're talking about, McLauren, is *he* with those knuckleheads?"

"I don't think he's hanging around anybody yet, far as I know."

"No Skin tattoos. That's a good sign."

This was the only thing he said that made me believe he'd at least read some of Lizzie's file. In the end, Hawk promised me he would talk to medical about him, which is all I can reasonably expect.

§

Back on the cellblock that evening, Panic eagerly waited until all the guards had left the area, then blurted out, "The eagle has landed! Get ready to fly through the fuckin' galaxy at warp speed." He was giggling like a mad scientist. My look of incomprehension made him quickly follow up with "The acid got in! Compliments of the ol' Axe Wound Moving Company."

"Oh." I'd forgotten about it.

"Are you in or what?" Panic asked.

"I still need all my brain cells. I've got legal work, remember."

"Your brain didn't help my appeal none! Just kiddin'. I knew it was a shot in the dark."

"I hope you enjoy it. Who's along for the ride?"

"Everybody 'cept old fuckers like you and Ed. Torch and Lars and them other weightlifters are pussies too. They don't put nothing in their bodies, you know."

"Are the new guys getting in on it?"

"Hell yeah. Master said there's a ton of it to go around. Scripts is only charging ten bucks a hit."

"I thought it was free. Part of his birthday celebration."

"Well, he's gotta recoup some import costs, they said."

"Ah, capitalism, gotta love it."

"This ain't about politics, man. This is about the brain-twist mind-fuck psychedelic parade. You ever done it?"

"No," I lied. "Never wanted to take the chance of messing up my wiring. It's bad enough as is."

"Listen, if you like them gummy bears you'll love this shit." So he knows. I guess I do act differently.

Grinning, I said, "I'll pass. I'm waiting to make sure it's a quality product."

"Oh, it's gonna be quality all right!"

"So lots of folks are in, huh?" I asked again. "Even losers like Skunk and newbies like Lizzie?"

"Master says that whole cellblock is in."

I snapped my fingers and sang, "Everybody, let's rock / Everybody in the whole cellblock/ Was dancin' to the jailhouse rock."

"Shit, there could be an Elvis sighting with this stuff, you dunno."

"Wouldn't surprise me a bit. How about the Skins? Are they in?"

"They're good to go, all around."

"Drugs will keep us together. Scripts is a good businessman. He'll sell to whoever. Maybe something good will come out of it." I lie down on my cot.

But what good could come of it? Perhaps race relations would improve if the Skinheads were tied up and forced to watch hours and hours of *Soul Train* while tripping, maybe they could learn to share the love.

Panic has no idea that I came of age in the late seventies listening to Pink Floyd and learning about windowpane and purple microdots, thanks to my older cousin. I can't think of anything worse than dropping acid in this shithole. It sounds like the recipe for a uniquely depressing, soul-shattering experience. I'm sure some of the participants will have a marvelous time laughing their asses off, but I suspect that not all are ready for what the LSD might unlock.

For example, I hope Panic is emotionally prepared for a flashback of his father killing his mother in the kitchen. He says he's dosed before and isn't concerned about it. But mostly I'm worried about Thin Lizzie, given his psychiatric profile. I don't think any reputable psychiatrist would recommend hallucinogens to cure his particular maladies. If he's truly searching for some type of redemption, as Miguel believes, he damn sure won't find it hanging around with Scripts and those guys.

In my youthful experimentation, I was fortunate to never have a bad trip. LSD is a drug best enjoyed outdoors in the church of nature.

When I was a junior in college, Gil came home for a visit and simply stated, "You're ready. It's time." We drove out to the farm where a combination of naïveté and blind trust caused me to extend my open palm, communion-style, and receive a tiny paper wafer that changed everything for me.

Gil said, "Your eyes will be very sensitive to light and you're going to sweat a lot. That's normal. I brought water. Relax." We walked around aimlessly all day. The farm was a feast of colors, the vibrancy of which I hadn't quite fathomed or appreciated before then. Every facet of the natural world—plant, animal, water, sky—was enhanced, interconnected, and exalted. I noticed the myriad greens and yellows of moss and lichen illuminated by lasers of sunlight. And I was especially attentive to a goldfinch dining atop thistle; it seemed like he was there for an eternity, and I felt supremely privileged that he didn't fly away. I marveled, slack-jawed, at the awkward-looking physics of my horse scratching his face with a back hoof—a common enough occurrence that I'd witnessed a hundred times and never thought a thing about. A flotilla of leaves from maple, oak, and hickory trees flowed down the creek, face up to the sun, drifting toward the waterfall. Downstream, those same reds and golds were plastered onto glistening rocks. *How, I wondered, had I taken all this for granted?*

I remember there was a cloud-filled, purple-pink sunset over the perfect mirror of the catfish pond, a scene which, years later, Emily would successfully capture in pastel, making it seem like my psychoactive journey somehow presaged my wife. Anything's possible. We don't know the half of it.

On that day, Gil and I returned to the innocence of our childhoods. This intense shared experience further strengthened our bond, making it seem unbreakable. Until our conviction.

I couldn't stop thinking about my having promised Miguel I would look out for Lizzie. What was the best way to do this? I mean, you can't keep people from doing things they really want to do, like drugs, can you?

I originally thought of relaying a message to Scripts through Panic since they're pals, but then I worried that it could somehow be misinterpreted as my rendering a legal opinion of some sort. I also considered having an avuncular talk with Lizzie, as I have from time to time with other younger inmates, but then I decided that his mental state was too precarious. I could've used Miguel's name as an entrée, but I didn't get the impression that Miguel had told Lizzie that Miguel and I were friends.

Still, I had to try something. I knew I would have to go directly to the source. Because of his monetary success, Scripts has become like a gang lord or Mafia kingpin. You're encouraged not to interact with him unless you need a favor or just want to publicly kiss the ring. I decided to approach him on the yard, which is the easiest place to talk to him these days. He's sinewy as a Navy Seal. His pale eyes are not level, the left being noticeably lower, giving him a feral look. Despite appearing more than capable of taking care of himself, he's always accompanied by two of his large lieutenants. Though I handled a few minor legal matters for some of his posse, I'd never done any work specifically for Scripts. By the time I arrived at Congaree, he had exhausted all of his appellate options. When he first asked me if there was anything I could do to help him out, I had to tell him no. I distinctly remember his disapproving stare.

As I walked toward Scripts, he nodded his head affirmatively, which I assumed meant it was okay for me to speak to him. We gave each other a fist bump.

"What can I do you for, Counselor?" He seemed jovial compared to the other times we'd conversed.

"I have a big favor to ask," I said.

"Shoot."

I summarized Thin Lizzie's history.

"So he's a Manson?" he said.

"No, no. He's not the evil kind. What I'm saying is I think he's too weak, mentally, to be doing acid. Not everybody can handle that stuff. I think he's one of them."

"Whoa, whoa. Remember, man, I don't know shit about no fuckin' LSD. That's the story. Got it?"

I hadn't considered the fact that I'd never discussed drugs directly with Scripts before, only his minions. Had they not told him that I'm clued in, and trustworthy as well? Maybe because I'm a lawyer, no one said anything.

"Oh, yeah. I understand. No worries with me." I said, raising my hands to shoulder height in a defensive gesture of assurance.

"What the hell's a dude like Lizzie doing in here anyway? I thought they kept the nutjobs crosstown."

"They still do. He slipped through the cracks. He's..." I was interrupted when one of Scripts' lieutenants came over and whispered in his ear. I didn't think it was about me because the man nodded in the direction of some other inmates fifteen yards away. The yard is where a majority of transactions take place.

When Scripts directed his attention back to me, I quickly got to the point. "All I'm asking is that he not be given anything. But I don't want anybody to be out any money so I'll pay whatever to make up for the loss. How much do I owe?"

"Nah, man." Scripts waved me off. "Keep the chump change. I'll survive. It's good to have a lawyer owing me one."

"So we're good?"

"That's it. Unless you can get me the fuck outta here."

"If I could, I'd get us both out."

I extended my fist for a parting bump but he'd already moved on to a more pressing matter.

Chapter 14

After Gil had been home a while, we got in the habit of meeting his buddy Charlie Reese for lunch once a week. Charlie preferred to go someplace upscale, befitting the president of the bank, but Gil resented country clubs, opting instead for Sonny's Bar & Grille, a blue-collar favorite on the outskirts of town. Originally, he'd told Charlie on the phone: "It's the best place in town to hear dialogue."

Charlie balked. "I thought the purpose was to eat. Have you seen their kitchen? It's sanitation grade is B. I shit you not."

"Don't wear a damn pink bow tie if you're planning on sitting with us." Gil laughed and hung up. "It's good for Charlie to get out of his comfort zone every now and then."

I always enjoyed going to Sonny's because it allowed me to fraternize with clients—past, present, and hopefully future. It was good PR for a defense attorney to be seen there, to let the hard-working guys know that you, unlike the doctors, weren't eating on white tablecloths all the damn time. I can't speak to the cleanliness of the kitchen, but the fries were great. On this day, the parking lot was full of pickups: beat-up, rusting Fords belonging to plumbers and construction outfits, a lawn-service Ram pulling a trailer loaded with mowers, and some newer model Chevys, one with a mud-splattered four-wheeler in the bed. Gil and I were riding together and running a little late. As we wove through the lot, it was easy to spot Charlie's sleek, silver Mercedes coupe. It was parked diagonally, ten yards away from the nearest vehicle.

"Look at that," Gil said. "The asshole's taking up three spaces."

Charlie was one of the few people who could make Gil laugh. It was a reciprocal friendship. They grew up hunting on the farm and Charlie was always invited to participate when Gil brought his New York buddies down for dove shoots. Charlie and I enjoyed watching Gil play the lord of the manor on those occasions, introducing the city boys to the pleasures of good moonshine and a bonfire. Once drunk, Charlie entertained us with dirty jokes, his knowledge encyclopedic.

Inside, I waved to some folks I knew, one of whom had been promising for a year to pay the remainder of my fee. I'd gotten him out of a serious hit-and-run; he was lucky to not be behind bars. I was pissed at him, which I very much regret now, for while I was awaiting my own trial, I received his full-balance payment along with a handwritten note wishing me well. People surprise you sometimes.

At noon on a Wednesday, it was crowded with regulars. Charlie, sporting a lavender tie, was sitting in a booth in the back section near the bar. Charlie glanced at me, then turned to Gil. Charlie had always been fond of using certain introductory phrases to signal his seriousness. Most of them would sound patronizing if spoken by anyone else, but because of Charlie's slow, smooth drawl, you felt as though he was patiently helping you work through a simple transaction at the bank.

"Realize something, Gil; you're not in the Big Apple anymore."

"Thanks. It's good to know I don't need a GPS when you're around," Gil said.

"Laugh all you want, but remember that I've got kids to raise in this town," Charlie said.

Gil cleared his throat but didn't say anything.

"There's no such thing as anonymity around here. It doesn't matter that you're living out at the farm."

"Sounds like you're determined to say what's on your mind. Have at it, dammit," Gil said.

"All right." Charlie began to whisper. "Everybody knows you're fucking that married woman in Logan County."

Briefly silenced, Gil quickly became defensive. "So you believe everything you hear? Is that it?"

"Not if you tell me it's a lie," Charlie said.

Gil would've been better off just fessing up right then, but he was still too surprised. In fact, I'm not sure who was more taken aback at the moment, Gil or me. How long had he been home, only three months? And this already?

"Who told you that?" Gil asked Charlie.

"You want them listed alphabetically?"

"I see. So it's bad?"

"Pretty scandalous. For *here* anyway."

"I can't believe people would care."

Charlie slowly shook his head. "Of course they do. Welcome home."

I looked at Gil and asked, "Does this mystery woman have a name?"

Charlie beat him to it. "Regina."

"Yeah. You seem to know everything," Gil said.

Later, when Gil went to the bathroom, Charlie launched into the details. "He's found himself a young cowgirl. Regina Crowder, thirty years old. She used to be on the barrel racing circuit for a while. Blue-collar horse world. This isn't some hunter-jumper sophisticate we're talking about. She could probably kick my ass. Damn, Jack, it's been like this his whole life."

"What more do you know about her?"

"Rich husband, much older. His family's got a big sand and gravel outfit in Georgia. Second marriage for both. Each has kids from the prior. None together. I hear she's got a full trophy case on display from her competition days." Charlie paused to dab his mouth fastidiously with a paper napkin. "Live in a McMansion. The million-dollar, climate-controlled barn was in some equine magazine you probably subscribe to. It has, like, twenty stalls. You'd think it belongs to the King of Dubai. And that gentleman there," he said, nodding toward Gil, who was walking back from the bathroom, "just happens to be servicing the King's wife. Shocker, right?"

I said, "I'll call you later. I wanna hear more."

"That's all I know."

"Still, I want to talk."

Charlie and I simultaneously sipped our sweet teas as Gil came up. "I'm sure you two have put a stop to all the nasty gossip going around."

"We were talking football. Don't flatter yourself," Charlie said.

Gil grabbed a pool stick off the wall and waved it at us as if wielding a fencing foil. "Got time for one game of eight ball?"

"Can't do it," Charlie said. "I've got a one o'clock."

Gil said, "Looks like it's me and you, Jackson. Mano-a-mano."

"We don't have time. We've got to meet Billy, remember," I said.

Charlie laughed and said, "Gil's got that busy work schedule, Jack. It's hard for him to keep track of it all."

I have long suspected that Charlie helps Gil out financially whenever the need arises. If true, it goes a long way toward explaining why Charlie feels so at liberty to criticize Gil's behavior.

Gil chalked his stick and broke the rack so hard that the cue ball flew off the table and rolled over by the jukebox. He polished off his PBR, then picked up the cue ball and nonchalantly threw it onto the table without bothering to look where it landed.

As we walked out into the sunlight, Charlie said, "*Damn it!*" He carefully lifted up his tie to get a closer look at a big grease stain.

"Highly unprofessional to walk around looking like that," Gil said, winking at me.

On the ride to the farm to meet Billy Alexander, Gil cut loose. "What's with that fucking lecture from Charlie? What a crock of self-righteous *bullshit!* Did you hear him? *'I have to raise kids in this town.'* What's *that* supposed to mean?" I'd rarely seen Gil with such bruised feelings. I think he was especially sensitive because Charlie's oldest child, David, is his godson. In the past, Gil has been good about having them up to New York for visits, occasionally scoring Yankees tickets.

"He was just messing with you. The way y'all always do," I said.

"No he wasn't. He was making a *statement*. Standing in judgment."

"What the hell is wrong with you? Charlie worships the ground you walk on."

"Not anymore, it doesn't sound like."

"Make no mistake, he did you a favor by saying something to you."

"Well..."

"When were you planning on telling me?" I asked.

"I made certain promises. I try to keep them. It wasn't a matter of not trusting you. You know how it is."

"How do you think people know?"

"The same way they always do. We've been careful, I can tell you that."

"Yeah, and every one of my drug dealers thought they were being careful before they got busted."

"What?" Gil was distracted, looking at the liner notes of my J. J. Cale CD.

"You haven't been out in public with her, have you?"

Reluctantly, he revealed that they had been to several different hotels in the Columbia area, never the same one and never driving together. He also admitted that he'd invited her out to the farm a few times. I thought about what an easy job it would have been for a private eye. I was furious with Gil for using the farm for his trysts, but I knew there was no use in even broaching that topic.

The wisdom that Gil had once imparted in his short stories about the unhappiness of a womanizer seemed completely lost on him. It was no big surprise. Events in his life were merely "research" anyway—something to be used later based upon its emotional resonance. And since females were his primary subject matter, this was quite easily accomplished. Think Fitzgerald writing compellingly about the ravages of alcoholism while he continued to drink.

"How did you meet this woman?"

"Believe it or not, at Tractor Supply." We both laughed.

"I guess there's a certain intrigue with long shots. Give me the details," I said.

"You expect me to gossip like everyone else?"

"Absolutely."

"I offered to carry a salt lick to her car, not that she needed help lifting it. She let me. We flirted, made jokes about licking."

"The consummate Southern gentleman. So what do you know about the husband?"

"He's a sadistic son of a bitch. Slaps her around when he gets drunk."

"How do you know that? Based on what she said?"

"She wouldn't lie," Gil said.

"Have you seen any marks or bruises?"

"No. He hasn't done it lately. Not since I've known her."

"What if he finds out about you?"

"You think I don't know the risk?"

"Well, how could you if you've never met the guy? Has she ever called the police to report the domestic abuse?"

"I'm not sure. I don't think so. She's scared of him."

"You don't *think* so? Basically, then, you've been doing a lot more fucking than talking."

"That's a little indelicate, but not inaccurate."

"Let me ask you this: Is she thinking about getting a divorce? I mean, has she talked to a lawyer about it?"

"Not that I know of."

"The husband is supposed to be loaded. Is there a prenup?"

"You're a born romantic, aren't you."

"Be serious."

"How can I ask her a question like that without sounding like a gold digger?"

"Have you considered that maybe *she* was one when she married him?"

"Ah fuck you, Jack. Since when did you and Charlie become the morality police?"

"Well, remember how freaked out you got thinking that Tina Mitchell's husband might hear about you."

"The coke made me paranoid," Gil said. "That was before rehab, you know."

After this, I backed off. Gil helped me get through the tough times with my mom, so I was indebted to him.

We were on Highway 42 approaching the Rocky Creek bridge, which marks the county line. I looked in my rearview mirror and saw that no one was behind me. I rolled down my window and slowed down, turning on my flashers just in case. It had rained the day before, and I wanted to hear the running water. I came to a complete stop and looked down. The water was flowing over the orange rocks, a smooth ribbon headed toward the Catawba River. The afternoon sun filtered through the tree limbs, casting a spiderweb of shadows onto the gray boulders that lined the banks of the creek. I couldn't see any deer or hawks or bobcats on this day, but I knew they were there watching me.

I turned my flashers off and accelerated.

"Still doing it," Gil said.

"I like traditions."

"A creature of habit for sure. Probably why you can't quit smoking."

The bridge was the line of demarcation between the townie life of my father's family and the country life of my mother's. Dad was very handy with a chipping wedge and a putter, but if he ever picked up a hammer or a shovel in his life, it was to hand it to some hired help. Despite the fact that Mom's family had made its money in town for two generations, they preferred country life. They were proud of the fact that their Scottish ancestors were farmers dating back before the Revolution-ary War. Since coming to America in 1772, they had grown cotton, corn, and soybeans, cultivated timber, and raised cows.

For most of my life, I had balanced country and city. If I went too long without seeing my mother's relatives, they would accuse me of being "one of those yuppies" or having "soft hands." When I spent a lot of time in the country, Dad's folks would start calling me a "hillbilly" and asking if I had any good tips on pig farming. This was all good-natured ribbing to be sure, but behind the playful insults was a certain posses-siveness.

As we approached the farm, Gil said, "Don't tell Emily."

"What if she hears it on the streets and knows I've held back on her?" I said, incredulous.

"How's she going to know? Act surprised."

"*She'll* know. You've been married, you know how it is."

We were only a few minutes late for our appointment. Billy had parked his car down by the catfish pond and was already looking around. I apologized for my tardiness despite knowing that Billy wasn't concerned about it. He was a grade between me and Gil in school and, as kids, we both had liked him. He is a sincere, cheerful country boy, which is why most people enjoy his company. He hadn't seen Gil in decades, probably since a funeral. He carried on, backslapping Gil a couple of times before asking what he was doing these days.

"Still writing."

"What's that book of yours about?"

"You name it, Billy. Everything, I guess." Gil shifted back and forth nervously from one leg to the other.

"You been workin' on it a long time, haven't you? How many darn pages is that thing up to now?" What made it so painfully awkward was that Billy was genuinely curious.

"A lot. I...I'm not sure exactly. But I'm close to the end. I hope."

"Well, I'm lookin' forward to reading it. I know it'll be a good 'un."

Billy has been working for the university's farm extension service since high school. He had helped me with many issues over the years. On this day, he was there to talk about the otter problem. I specifically wanted Gil present so he could see the upkeep required to maintain the paradise that he awakened to every morning. For the first time ever, otters had gotten into the pond over winter and killed all of my catfish. Gil learned things he did not know, namely, that otters come from nearby creeks and can run as fast as humans. It's easy for them to kill the catfish in winter because the fish are slower.

"Otters are some tough sons a bitches," Billy said. "We can trap and move 'em, which'll cost you. Or I can shoot them. But that don't mean others won't come back next winter for the easy pickings. Word's out now."

"Every species gossips," Gil noted.

As with so much else in life, there were no good solutions to the otter problem. One of my earliest memories was of fishing in that pond with my grandfather. He used to feed the catfish huge bags of dried dog food to keep them fat and happy. It was hard to believe they were gone. I offered to pay Billy for the assessment, which he kindly refused, and I told him we'd have to think about the options. Gil and I made a promise to get together with him for a beer in the near future, which we knew would never happen.

I was grateful the otters hadn't made it to the bass ponds. Since Gil was unemployed, maybe he could be in charge of fending off the otter invasion.

After Billy left, we walked over to the barn. I recall that the early spring weather was ideal. I put Gil on Scout, my most sure-footed horse. I had to check that Scout was cinched up tight enough because Gil was obviously out of practice. I laid the ground rules down up front: We would, at most, occasionally canter, no galloping. I knew Gil was unlikely to abide by this, so I lied and said that Scout had recently pulled a chest muscle and I didn't want to risk re-injury.

We decided to ride the circumference of the property. I needed to check on some fencing in the northeast pasture anyway. Early on, for his own safety, I told Gil, "You're leaning forward like you're scared to death you'll fall. To be honest, it's an *ugly* seat. I don't think your girl-friend will be too impressed when she sees you in the saddle."

Gil said, "I taught your ass how to ride a goddamn horse."

"Well, sit back in the saddle then like you know what the hell you're doing. If Scout trips, you'll go flying over his head."

A while later, when he thought I wasn't looking, he shifted to the rear of the saddle and straightened his back, his new black cowboy boots gleaming in the afternoon sun. I couldn't help but notice that his feet were too far up in the stirrups, but I didn't say anything. If he got dragged a ways, it might knock some sense into him. All told, it had been a pretty tough day for the G-Man, mostly the realization that his affair was public knowledge but also Billy's innocent inquiry about his book.

We doubled back to the south fork of Rocky Creek, where we'd seen the panther as kids. The sun was setting. A small, sandy beach had been created where the stream doglegged sharply left. Some of the trees growing beside the creek had intricate root systems clinging stubbornly to the bank. Underneath a canopy of oaks, sycamores, and beech trees, we ground-tied the horses by the water. I often went to these woods alone to think about my cases. Why, I would wonder, had I chosen such a sad profession, one with pain and loss at its very core? Hadn't I had enough of that already?

I tried to coax Gil into talking about Regina, but he wouldn't have any part of it. He didn't want to talk about serious matters, he said.

Fifty yards downstream, I noticed that an ancient live oak had blown over in the previous week's high winds. It had fallen parallel to the creek, never crossing over the curving boundary of the bank. The same creek water that had sustained the tree eventually undermined it. Gil and I walked over to look at the eight-foot rootball, an earthen tangle of roots, worms, and shards. I spotted a carefully crafted, three-inch quartz arrowhead. When I reached for it, Gil was angry that he hadn't seen it first.

We walked to what was, for some three-hundred years, the top of the tree. The upper limbs were covered with lime-colored lichen. Now, I thought, it would be possible for flightless animals to finally perch atop the tree, scanning the ground for both predator and prey.

Before leaving the farm, I put the arrowhead on the kitchen counter beside the refrigerator where Gil couldn't miss it.

Chapter 15

On a Tuesday around noon I surprised Gil and his lady friend at the barn. I had some downtime at the office and rode out to check on my horse Midnight, who was stalled with a stone bruise, which I'd been soaking in Epsom salts for days. The metal gate was open and I saw a shiny Exxis horse trailer parked by the persimmon tree. It was too expensive to belong to horse thieves.

I would've preferred that Gil ask me before bringing strange horses around Midnight, who would sometimes get nervous around ones he didn't know, especially when stalled. I didn't want him frantically pacing, worsening his bruise. Fortunately, my older horse, Scout, grazing in the pasture, ignored the drama.

In the aisle, two gorgeous Peruvian Pasos were tethered to wooden posts. Standing between them, Gil had a sheepish grin to go along with his brand-new Stetson straw hat. I found myself wishing that he looked as ridiculous to others as he did to me, but I guess he wore it well, because just then a long-haired blonde descended the hayloft stairs. Her Wrangler jeans, at my eye level, were skin tight. She wasn't wearing a hat.

As I watched her, I fed Midnight a carrot and rubbed his white blaze. He nickered calmly. I figured Gil must have been there awhile, long enough for Midnight to adjust.

Gil said, "Regina, this is my cousin Jack I've told you about." Her handshake was as firm as any man's.

"How d'ya like Gil's hat I got him?" She had a serious Southern drawl.

"It's a keeper," I said. "But it'll need some sweat stains so he won't look like a city boy."

"Don't you worry. I'm gonna get that boy to break a sweat," she said smiling.

"We were getting ready to saddle up," Gil said. "You're just in time to help with the tack."

"Don't hurt your back lifting them saddles, Gilly," Regina said laughing. She then grabbed a pick and bent over to clean the hooves of one of her Peruvians. I had a splendid view, and Gil caught me looking.

The decorative saddle that I carried probably cost over three thousand. It had RDC tooled into the leather on the seat jockey.

When I walked back in the barn, Regina had placed a red saddle blanket on her horse. It also had her initials on it, stitched in black in the bottom right corner. She grabbed the saddle from me saying, "I'll take it from here. If you get me those bridles, too, I'll love you forever. Gilly's still fooling around with his saddle."

I fetched them for her. I heard them laughing loudly in the barn, but they were quiet when I returned. Regina chose the bridle she wanted. Her short fingernails were painted the same red color as her saddle blanket. I draped the other bridle over a stall door near Gil's horse.

Old wooden nameplates of my grandfather's former horses were still nailed to the four stall doors: Toby, Blue, Ranger, and Doll. One of my earliest memories was helping Grandad put salve on Blue's leg wounds after he got tangled up in barbed wire. The nameplates were nothing fancy, just half-inch pine painted white, with Gran's distinctive handwriting in burgundy. There was a thin layer of dust on them. The horses themselves were also nothing fancy, but they were reliable, sure-footed, and had no phobias or bad habits. Gran, like Emily, was never a horse person and always fretted about the safety of her husband and grandsons when they were riding.

At the age of sixty-seven, my grandad built this timber frame barn with the help of his contractor brother and two friends. All the lumber used in its construction came from oak trees on the property. He included several touches of mortise-and-tenon just for show. Remarking on the integrity of the barn's structure and the bulk of its beams, he once bragged that it would stand for a hundred and fifty years. It just might. I put on a new metal roof, but never had to do any structural work. The inside had basically remained untouched since the day Grandad died. I purposely kept it like a museum.

Even though I knew, I asked Regina, "So tell me about these Peruvians. I hear they're four-gaited."

"That's right. They're Pasos. I tell you what, these beauties ride smoother than my new Audi. You ever been on one?"

"A few times. They're impressive, but a little small for a tall guy to spend money on."

Regina said, "They're tough, though. Durable on the trail and fearless."

"Did you train them?"

"Oh, no. I only know barrel racers. We got some guru in Florida to do it. Now your boy there..." She nodded toward Midnight in his stall. "He's kinda high strung."

"Yeah, he doesn't get a lot of socialization out here."

"What's he stalled for?"

"Got a bad stone bruise. Did you notice a limp?"

"Nope. He was skittish when we got here, but I calmed him down good and quick. Just 'cause he's a gelding doesn't mean he should go without a woman in his life." She walked over and gave Midnight an apple wedge from a sandwich bag, then stroked his nose lightly with the front of her tanned fingers. I noticed a few strands of straw in the back of her hair. No doubt she'd checked her clothes thoroughly, but I imagine it was difficult to get all the straw out of that thick hair, especially in a hurry. She turned and walked back to her waiting Paso.

"What are their names?" I asked.

"This one's Ranger and Gilly's is Storm Signal. They both gotta be gettin' close to four now. Came from the same breeder up in Virginia. And they love each other to death." Regina seemed to be a big fan of the word *love*.

"So the breeder and the trainer were different?"

"Yeah. And now a different rider. The horse world's gone corporate 'cause of the Internet. Ah shit, forgot my hat. Gilly, be a dear and get that for me. I think it's in the front seat of the truck." I extended my hand to hold his reins for him.

Regina got in the saddle. I've been around a lot of horsewomen in my life, but I've never seen anyone mount a horse as gracefully as she did. Gil returned with a Stetson exactly like his. They'd already graduated to his and hers attire.

"If I'm not back in a few hours, don't send a search party out for me," Gil said. He snickered and tipped his hat down slightly. He was starring in his own movie.

"Hope we get to see each other again soon!" Regina said.

"Me too. Try not to get him killed."

She clicked her tongue and the Peruvian obediently trotted off, Gil following.

I went back down to soak Midnight's hoof. As I knelt in the stall bedding, firmly holding Midnight's leg still with both hands, the smell of pine shavings made me nostalgic, as it always did. I thought of how often Gil and I used to ride horses together as kids and how abruptly he opted for the city "to become a writer." I thought of Gil's ex-wife Hannah, comparing her to Regina. Shy, bookish, and unpretentious, Hannah was a native Brooklynite who taught eighth-grade English. To me, she always seemed happiest curled up on the window seat of their Bleecker Street apartment, wearing her baggy pajamas, and poring over student papers. But when we went out at night, she would let her long black hair down from the twist, throw on a simple black dress and, within minutes, transform herself into a dazzling beauty. But I think Gil loved her for her mind as much as anything. For his birthday one year, she found a first edition of Issac Babel's *Red Calvary*. He tried to give it back to her in the divorce, but she wouldn't take it. Hannah had just started to do some editing work for a publishing house when she and Gil split up. I never knew if these two events were somehow related.

That night when I got home, I told Emily about Regina. I didn't have the answer to most of her questions. She suspected that I was holding something back. I finally said, "How much can you tell about someone in thirty minutes?"

"Well, what was your impression of her. Other than new money?"

"I don't have one."

"Come on."

"Okay. She wears too much makeup."

"That's *it*?

"And she calls him Gilly."

"*Gilly*? Ha! You tell him I'm going to start calling him Gilligan then!"

"I'll let you tell him."

"Seriously. How long do you think this little fling will last?"

"Not long," I lied for some unknown reason.

§

After seeing Gil with Regina, I knew he would try to be around her as much as he possibly could. The thrill of their new relationship was not likely to wear off any time soon. I also knew that it wouldn't be long before her husband heard the rumors, if he hadn't already. He probably had a P.I. tailing her. I couldn't help but wonder if the husband was abusive, for all I had to go on was Gil's word. Yet the legal profession makes you expect the worst. I enlisted my ex-cop pal, Ron Patton, now a private investigator for the defense, to find out everything there was to know about Mr. Crowder—his criminal record, ownership of registered firearms, net worth, daily routines, and so on. Ron said it would take about two months to do it right. I appreciated his meticulous work, which in the past had successfully sent so many of my clients to prison. I was glad Ron switched to my side. He had always possessed the two traits that defense attorneys fear most in a cop: honesty and intelligence.

Chapter 16

Scripts' birthday party came and went. On my cellblock, all participants seemed to enjoy themselves. There was much hysterical laughter, a vision or two, a serious discussion about the existence of God between Skunk and Fleet (both believers), an intense disagreement among several people about who is the most beautiful woman in the world (apparently, there could only be one), and more than a few jokes at young Ditto's expense.

Then the singing began. A native of the Lone Star State, Panic repeated the chorus of "Luckenbach, Texas" so many times that Easy Ed, not one to get irritated, finally had to scream at him. The revelers also sang happy birthday to Scripts even though he's on another cellblock and couldn't hear. I had to go to sleep with my earbuds in.

At breakfast the next morning, we learned that things were not as fun in cellblock D. Big C was visibly shaken when he described Lizzie's night to us:

"That boy was moanin' and groanin' something awful. Cryin' and hollerin' for his wife. Bonnie...Bonnie. *Then he started bangin' his head on the john!* Over and over. I couldn't believe it. I swear, he done it ten, fifteen times. *Hard.*"

Booker, also in D block, said, "That was some bad shit, Jack, I ain't kiddin'. Lizzie was freakin' the brothers *out*. They was all fucked up and got rattled. Thought it was some fuckin' psycho stuff goin' down. Long night, man, looong night. We tried to talk Lizzie down, but he just kept on. Over and over. Kept bangin'. That's when I called for the guards. Shoulda done it sooner."

Torch picked at his food without eating. He simply said, "We didn't wanna get nobody in trouble. We didn't know he was gonna do *that*. I seen it. I can't stop thinkin' about it, man."

Turns out it was sometime after 2 a.m. when Lizzie began slamming his head against the metal toilet until he was unconscious. They rushed him to Richland Memorial. The rumor is he's in critical condition with a fractured skull. Lizzie had suffered the same type of injuries as Eric Crowder.

In addition to being really pissed off, I felt like I had let Miguel down.

"Who gave him the drugs?" I asked.

"Master the one in charge," C said.

Master was sitting at the next table. When I saw that he was finished eating, I went over and asked if I could talk to him alone. He said sure and slid down the table away from his dining partners. I have a good relationship with him, due in part to my reviewing his trial transcript and suggesting certain appellate issues, which his lawyer agreed with and included in his brief. (Like me, Master's still waiting to hear from the higher court.) All I've asked in return for my services is a little protection. It's not like he has to do much. With the Firm as my first team, he gets to sit safely on the bench and watch until needed. I've always considered the fact that Master is one of Scripts' lieutenants to be a positive thing. Knowledge is power, and since he loves to gossip, I usually hear early on about what's happening in the importation business, and thus know a lot about the habits of my fellow inmates.

His blue eyes have the piercing intensity of a Van Gogh self-portrait. I'll bet he intimidated the jurors in his trial. Appearances matter in a court of law, and he *looks* like the kind of guy who would shoot two people in a drug deal. I'm glad he likes me.

In order to set the proper tone, I called him by his real name, Tim, signaling both familiarity and seriousness.

"I hear y'all had an exciting block party," I said.

"Gives headbanger new meaning, don't it?" Master said, yawning. "Sure hope that fucker's okay. You shoulda seen the blood in his cell. *Holy fuck.* Looked like ten people got massacred in there. Scared the shit out of the brothers, I'll tell you that. Hell, scared me too. Every time Lizzie hit his head, I saw mine exploding. Major buzzkill."

"Let me ask you something, Tim. Did Scripts or anybody else ever tell you not to give Lizzie any acid. Did they warn you about him being nuts?"

"No. Nobody told me dick. I sold to whoever had the cash, same as always. Why? Is this turning into some legal shit or something?"

"Not that I know of."

"So why ask me that? I mean, he only did *one* tab."

I told him about my conversation with Scripts, which maybe I shouldn't have, but I didn't want to lie.

I ended with "I'm sure it was just a misunderstanding. Scripts probably thought you got the word. I should've said something to you myself."

I had no illusions that Master would keep our conversation confidential, so I didn't waste my time asking him to. I was reasonably sure he wasn't lying. We've played a lot of poker and I know his tells.

"Don't be broadcastin' that Lizzie got it from me, okay. Especially if that fucker croaks. You're the lawyer, connect the dots. Know what I mean?"

"Yes. I don't think there's anything to worry about, Tim. You're not responsible."

This seemed to reassure him, and Master immediately started talking about tripping again soon, this time without the distraction.

§

I've never been good at disguising my frustration. It is, I believe, one of the failings that kept me from being a first-rate lawyer. I always admired my Uncle Robert's ability to keep his composure under the most stressful circumstances, a skill that his son and I would have been wise to emulate.

With this in mind, I tried to prepare myself for seeing Scripts on the yard. There was a fine line between making a valid point and causing trouble for myself. I remembered that Scripts killed his victim with a crossbow, stuffed the body into a steel drum, and burned it. Supposedly, the man had swindled Scripts' brother out of 30k.

I approached him slowly, casually.

"I thought we had a deal about Lizzie?" I said.

"Yeah, I don't know what happened, dude," he said nonchalantly. "I guess Master didn't get the memo. Not sure who didn't pass the word along." It sounded like the plausible deniability of a corporate executive.

"Have you heard through your contacts whether he's going to live?" I asked.

"Is it that bad?"

"He cracked his skull. That means his brain is swollen."

"Jeez, what a crazy motherfucker. Sounds like he didn't have much brains to begin with."

I remained silent.

"Hey listen," Scripts continued. "Can I get you to look over a letter one of my boys got from his lawyer? We ain't sure what this fucker's tryin' to say."

"Sure." I admit I didn't sound very enthusiastic.

"You want any of the blotter? It's on the house."

"No thanks."

"Y'sure? This shit's killer."

"I'm too old for that."

"Man, this stuff's like pussy; you're never too old for it."

"When you line up some of that, you let me know."

About then the guards started yelling for us to get in line so we could file back inside for dinner. Everything's done by inmate number. Troll is very strict about it so he can get a proper head count. When I turned to walk away, Scripts said, "Hey, Counselor. Don't forget how Lizzie got his nickname. He wasn't no fuckin' choirboy, you know."

There was nothing to do but keep on walking.

§

My timing was terrible.

The day after I talked to Scripts on the yard, the guards searched his cell. It certainly wasn't the first time. They know he's the source. They found nothing. He's too smart to have anything stashed there. Out of a sense of egalitarianism, I suppose, Hawk and his men also searched every cell on Scripts' block, eventually finding the mother lode. In two separate cells belonging to Scripts' most trusted lieutenants—Slow Eye and Boll Weevil—officers found what was rumored to be three weeks' worth of drugs for the entire unit, including the remainder of the acid and a pharmacy of opioids.

The drugs were inside their mattresses. As is customary, they claimed it was planted by unspecified enemies. Both culprits were sent to the hole for an extended stay. There was no way to smuggle drugs into solitary because none of the guards down there were on the take then. Since Boll Weevil and Slow Eye were both seriously addicted to Oxy-Contin, theirs will be a painful cold turkey in isolation.

§

"Lizzie's cell is haunted," Booker said.

I was in the main hallway sweeping when he saw me and stopped to talk.

"When did he die?" I asked, laying my broom aside.

"Nah, he still alive. Far as I know."

"What makes you say his cell is haunted then?"

"Hawk was remindin' me. Boy used to live there long time ago killed himself. Ten years now, maybe more. They found him hangin' by an electric cord. I know you don't believe, but it's true. Cell 419 is haunted. I ain't goin' near it. Never again. And you oughtn't neither, Jack."

He quickly left. I stared at my broom. Ghost stories unnerved me.

§

Lunchtime.

Panic, Torch, Lars, Booker, Easy Ed, and Big C sat around me at the dining table looking like solemn committee members facing an unpleasant task. I thought they were going to tell me that Lizzie had died. Instead, they told me there was a rumor that I was a snitch for the guards in this drug drama with Lizzie. The rumor was supposedly started by the Skins, Ed said. I could only hope my look of bafflement put to rest any suspicions my friends might have that such nonsense was true, for I knew all too well the Congaree truism "snitches get stitches."

I said, "That's not funny." The guys seemed to be waiting for me to say more, so I did. "What a crock of shit. Is this because I'm upset about Lizzie or what?" I heard my voice crack a little. Not wanting to protest too much, I shut up.

Panic said, "This is just payback for that ping pong shit. The Skins want you outta the way 'cause you side with Torch and Lars. They're recruiting all the dumbass rednecks. Wanna start the race war. Get rid of the Firm."

"*Are* there rednecks dumber than you?" Big C said.

"Very funny," Panic said, smiling. "You say that right when I'm on the fence about goin' over to their side. Remember I got no blacks in my family tree."

"That you know of," C said.

Their conversation quickly devolved into a pissing contest, until Easy Ed wisely brought the focus back to my current problem. "I don't think there's anything to worry about. It doesn't take a genius to figure out there's not a snitch in this situation. Only someone who's really high on dope would bang their head against a toilet. Lizzie might die, so Hawk probably got the drug screen from the hospital and that was that. By law, they had to do a search." Why couldn't everyone in this prison realize that my man Ed was the voice of reason?

Booker said, "Awright. Torch and C will tell the brothers you ain't no snitch. That it's just more Skins bullshit." I immediately felt a sense of relief, but then C followed up with "Still, lotta brothers gone be hurtin' for drugs. Might be lookin' for someone to blame when they strung out."

Ed looked at me and said, "C, the best thing you can do is tell your people that it's a Skin who's really the snitch and those assholes are trying to pull a fast one on Counselor."

The men all looked at me. I had to say something. "Whatever works. But I'm no *fucking* snitch and I don't want to go down because of this crap." I've made a lot of arguments in my life, but none more important than this. If my buddies don't believe me, then I'm doomed. Simple as that. A snitch is the one thing you absolutely *cannot* be in here, especially about drugs, which are the lifeblood of this dungeon.

After lunch, on the way back to our cellblock, I thanked Ed.

"A place like this," he said, "it's not enough to just deny something like that. You gotta give 'em somebody else to blame. But you need to watch your back. Stay close to Torch. It'll be good optics."

"Have you ever been in a situation like this, Ed?"

"Hell no. I don't run my mouth like you do."

§

When I got back to my cell, I ate half a gummy. One reason inmates who don't know me might be inclined to believe I'm a snitch is because I've been able to work my way up the job ladder pretty quickly. I started out in the laundry, which, other than cleaning toilets, is the worst job—tiring, hot, and loud, which means you cannot hear if someone is sneaking up on you. Because of my diligence and hard work, I was quickly moved up to kitchen detail, which is a little better but still tiring, hot, and frustrating. The guards closely monitor you to make sure you don't steal something that can be turned into a shiv.

It was in the kitchen that I first befriended Booker, who was supervising the floor clean-up detail. He liked that I was washing dishes while singing along to James and Bobby Purify. That's when we started talking seriously about music and realized how similar our tastes in R&B were. I quickly parlayed my burgeoning friendship with Booker into much better jobs. I am deeply indebted to him. Once he told Hawk and Troll that I was trustworthy—"This one ain't lookin' to steal anything or hurt nobody."—I was able to land the coveted position of hallway sweeper, which meant low effort, broad access, and social opportunities. You get to meet passersby and shoot the shit. This was how I came to be friends with the Firm and Easy Ed, who were also sweepers. It wasn't like I was an actual trusty yet like Booker, but it was a good start. For me, the ultimate goal was to work outside on the grounds crew where I could see the sky.

The truth is there are a lot of reliable inmates who've been here longer than me who are still working shitty jobs. It's only natural they should be jealous as well as curious about my rapid rise within the prison hierarchy. Since I'm gregarious and genuinely like some of the guards, I am often seen conversing with them. A natural assumption would be that I am an informant. As a trial attorney, I know that if people really *want* to believe something, all you have to do is give them a tiny morsel and repeat it over and over. Obviously, the dumber the person, the smaller the morsel required to get the job done.

Later, when the paranoia really took hold, I thought about my former client Hank Cranfill, who snitched on members of the notorious Skull and Bones biker gang. The case involved crystal meth, stolen motorcycles, and chop shops. Having a wife and kids, Hank couldn't see himself doing ten years in the federal pen, so he chose to cooperate with the U. S. Attorney's office in return for a nominal sentence. Most of his co-defendants were looking at upwards of twenty years. Though not actually a member of the gang, Hank prided himself on being a tough guy in their orbit, a hanger-on. He was brawny, covered with ink, and always wore biker boots, a black leather vest, and a long silver chain attached to the wallet in his back pocket. He startled the female staff at my law firm, a reaction he appeared to relish.

Behind the door of my conference room, Hank complained continually about the risks he'd be facing in prison and afterward because of his decision. The U. S. Attorney assured us that Hank would be segregated from his co-defendants during the six months he was incarcerated, and according to the records I reviewed in a subsequent civil suit, he was. Skull and Bones got to him anyway. A third-party assassin stuck a shiv in Hank on the yard, severing his ascending aorta, causing him to bleed out in minutes. If they want you bad enough, they'll get you. The rumor was they paid the assassin's family 20K. This is why some of my drug clients never snitched and thus did major time. But when they walked out, they did not have to look over their shoulders.

Uncle Robert got a good settlement for Hank's family. His wife sent us a Christmas card the first year when she still had some money left, before she started doing crystal meth and gambling in Biloxi. Her husband's assailant didn't face the death penalty.

I couldn't sleep. Throughout the night, I constantly checked my cell door to make sure it was still locked. The next morning I resolved to quit eating gummies for a while so I could reduce my paranoia and be more aware of my surroundings. I needed to be able to tell the difference between a real threat and an imaginary one. I knew that quitting would deepen my depression, but worrying about the threat is almost as bad as having the threat carried out. I'd just have to feel like shit to survive.

Most likely, I knew, I would be killed. And what of it? Wasn't I the guy who spoke so cavalierly about my disappointment when the prison doctor told me I was in good health? So what had changed? Death at the hand of another seemed more respectable than suicide, although I thought suicide required enormous courage.

Why was I scared? Was it the fear of death itself, of my extinction? Was it the fear of the pain that accompanied most violent deaths?

I suddenly remembered being a little kid playing with my neighborhood friend Tommy Hipps. Tommy and I discussed what would be the best way to die, as well as the most exciting way to kill someone else. Tommy firmly believed that a tomahawk to the head was the coolest way to go. He had one that his parents bought from some novelty store. The rock, painted a garish bright red, was tied to the shellacked wooden handle with crisscrossing leather. Thinking back, that tomahawk was about the same weight as a tire tool.

I doubt even Scripts' enterprising cartel can smuggle a tomahawk into Congaree, much less a gun. On rare occasions they've been able to gain access to a knife, whether from the outside or the kitchen. But being stabbed by a shiv is the most likely scenario. Inmates are ingenious, making them out of everything from broken glass to electrical wiring to plastic toothbrushes sharpened to an edge.

The only one I've seen was a shard of glass with a duct tape handle. I found it when I was sweeping behind a trash can near the rec room. I alerted the guards because I feared someone might use it against me or my friends and I didn't want to get caught possessing it, which gets you six months in the hole. Is this considered snitching? Does anyone know about it? I now wish I'd kept it for protection. I do have a hollowed-out hardback book in my cell that Beef never looks at during his obligatory searches. He's sure I'm clean. It's where I keep my gummies, and there's plenty of room inside for a shiv.

Then, there's the garrote to worry about. Guitar strings and piano wire have occasionally made their way inside as part of the arms race. Not that they're necessary. All it takes is cuffs, as that Skin tried with Torch. I fear suffocation most. Rumor has it that an inmate at another prison got strangled with a towel while working in the laundry room.

Me, I'd prefer some big guy breaking my neck. Snap, over. Quick and easy.

§

I've been on the john all morning. Regulation 18(c): "An inmate may stay in his cell due to sickness for a maximum of 24 hours without leaving, after which time if he continues to feel poorly, he must go to the infirmary." There's a good possibility that my absence from daily routines will cause some inmates to believe I'm avoiding interaction. After all, I live in a world where fear and guilt are often mistaken for each other. There's not much I can do about it, except hope that my friends can convincingly argue my case by mentioning that I had to bum some extra toilet paper from Panic. It doesn't get more legit than that.

§

This morning I had a revelation: *I will do something that gets me sent to the hole.* I'll leave some drugs out in plain view for Beef to see. Then I'll be safe in solitary for a while. The guards wouldn't bust their own snitch, right?

I was so excited about my new plan that I told Panic, who quickly scuttled it: "People gonna think you're in some kinda witness protection shit that the guards control, you being in the hole just a big lie. The Skins could make people think you're livin' in some secret place with a private shower and cable TV, havin' pizza delivered."

Panic knows the way these people think. I defer to his opinion.

Critical question: Should I tell the guards about what's going on with this snitch rumor? The carefully considered answer—and one I'm not entirely comfortable with—is *no*, because if they appear to be protecting me in any way, it could reinforce someone's belief that I'm actually working with them. Much as I hate it, it's too risky to get Hawk, Troll, or Beef involved.

Given the time spent pondering this snitch business, it's possible that I might be going a little nuts. I need a break. I haven't been able to think about anything else for days, evidenced by the number of pages in my journal that I've filled with different flow charts concerning potential scenarios. I think my legal training is becoming a curse.

§

On Tuesday, Beef told us Brian McLauren passed away. The doctors couldn't relieve the pressure. It's probably a blessing. Lizzie would have been a vegetable. The only legal question now is whether the coroner will classify his death as a suicide, an overdose, or an accident (most likely under the heading of "misadventure"). I doubt there will be a thorough investigation into the death of an axe murderer.

Lizzie's mother has made arrangements for the body to be shipped to Idaho, where she lives. At this point, no matter who you were or what you did with your life, it becomes a matter of logistics. Take Chekhov, for example: When he died of consumption in the Black Forest at the age of 44, his body was transported to Moscow in a refrigeration car used for hauling oysters.

Miguel isn't due to visit for another week. It is conceivable he might not know the news until then, unless Hawk calls him. Because of my initial conversation with Miguel, I feel culpable for Lizzie's death. I also feel like I've let down the one person I admire around here. Yet I will tell him about how Lizzie died. I owe Miguel the truth.

Chapter 17

I wasn't being nosy. I happened on them by chance. But I doubt she'll ever believe that. Emily handled our financial matters, and on this day I had to look through her emails to find some information that our stockbroker had sent. That's when I noticed how many she'd received from a certain dgundy@artsolutions.net. There were over three hundred within three months. At first I was baffled, but after reviewing a number of them, I finally figured out they were from her Charleston friend Douglas Gunderson. I gleaned that he was serving as president of some statewide board of art therapists.

I hadn't seen this guy since our wedding, though I'd occasionally heard his name mentioned when Emily and her sisters talked about people from Charleston. No big deal. But what concerned me now was the fact that I hadn't heard his name more often over the years.

After an unfulfilling decade of teaching art in a local private academy, Emily had decided to go back to school to become a certified art therapist. Unsurprisingly, she was great at her new job. Initially, it enhanced her sense of self-worth in ways I doubt even she had imagined. She resembled the spunky Emily of old, excited about the possibility of each new day. But then, over time, therapy became a grind, a predictable outcome given her tendency to get too emotionally involved with the children. She began to display the same distraction that she'd often noticed in me because of the law. I still believe Emily needed some therapy of her own as a result of what she saw and heard, but she would never acknowledge this. Emily and I were bringing our stressful work back home at the end of long days.

Emily often had seminars, workshops, and meetings in Charleston, where she saw "Sylvia and Donna and the gang." But I don't remember her ever mentioning Douglas's name when she talked about those trips. I'd always considered myself above such self-defeating nonsense as jealousy. Since I had a younger, attractive wife, it always seemed like it would be bad form to show the slightest inkling of possessiveness. Yet it was always there.

I read all of their emails to each other. Since they corresponded multiple times daily, it took me the better part of a rainy Saturday to go through them the first time. I felt like I was reading each one's diary, complete with their feelings on family, work, and art. They frequently discussed Douglas's painful divorce the year before. He often mentioned how agonizing it was that he got to see his six-year-old son only every other weekend. Emily's responses alternated between those of a friendly colleague and of a concerned older sister who was willing to give the occasional lecture.

Some of his emails were cloying. I couldn't believe that someone like Emily would welcome or encourage them, but since they'd grown up together, I knew full well that a childhood connection creates its own dynamic.

There was no mention of sex, or anything overtly flirtatious, but no married man ever wants his wife to bond with another man unless he's a close family member. She already had her two sisters, whom she talked to constantly. I factored into the equation that Emily would've felt very sorry for Douglas about his marital breakup. I even considered the possibility that he was the brother that she never had growing up in a house full of women. He must have reminded Emily of her youth in Charleston, a time when she still thought she could have children of her own. Perhaps a happier time.

Their emails revealed that Emily was starved for attention, which frankly shocked me. It was obvious that he worshipped my wife and had become emotionally dependent on her. But what hurt me the most, initially, was the fact that Emily had granted someone else a window into the life we had worked so hard to build.

Upon my second reading of their messages, everything was cast in a different light. With each successive email, I could feel his attempt to unravel my marriage. Painful as it was to reread the crucial ones, I couldn't stop myself.

Had his tireless efforts ultimately proved successful? When I finally asked her about the emails, Emily said coolly, "Jack, I *told* you Douglas was in the therapy crowd. You just don't listen to me when I'm talking. You're a million miles away."

But I couldn't help but play the lawyer with my newfound evidence. I read two of the emails to her. Emily had her back to me, busily washing dishes and laying them in the drain board. The first email was from her:

November 12

D.— Thanx bunches for the referral. Little Andrea is PRECIOUS. Based on my sessions with her and Ben, I feel like I could have been a decent mother. I know how much time you've put in these last few months. We all marvel at how patient you are with Dave. You have a rare and true gift, and we love you for it!

Douglas responded immediately.

Believe me, you would be the best mom ever! And that's what you are to these kids in more ways than one. I saw Ben's folks at dinner the other night and they were raving about how wonderful you are. No surprise to me.

Are you coming down on Thurs. or Fri.? Staying at your folks or hotel? Sylvia said we're having drinks at her place one night. Can't wait. Drive safely. Be sure to play that Winehouse song "Wake Up Alone" on the way down. Great stuff.

"It's also very sexy stuff, don't you think?" I said. "There was no response to his questions, that I found. So I guess that was all done over the phone, huh?"

Emily still had her back to me. Her voice cracked a little when she said, "For heaven's sake, you're being paranoid! That's just work chat. You're cherry-picking stuff. You hang out with lawyers all the time, so stop it, Jack."

But I wasn't done yet. Not even close. I read another one from her that really stung. Then I asked, "Was that just work chat too?"

She was silent. Her shoulders began to rise, then lower before rising again. She turned off the water faucet and spun around, her face glistening with tears.

She said, *"I've never done anything with him!"*

I grabbed my coat and walked out the back door into the dark. Her intensity said it all.

It was a lot colder outside than I thought. I needed a heavier coat and gloves but I wasn't about to go back inside. At least I had smokes in my pocket. To stay warm, I quickly started walking down the street, unsure of when I might stop.

Smoke, think, walk. Inhale for two steps. Exhale for four.

There was comfort in the sureness of my stride, and I hoped that this familiar rhythm would somehow offset the loss of equilibrium I felt in my marriage.

I slowed to light another cigarette and suddenly realized how far I had walked. Not paying attention, I'd gone almost all the way across town to the abandoned textile mill. I knew how suspicious it would look if a cop saw me there at that time of night. The last thing I needed was a rumor going around that I was looking to score in Crack Town. I jogged back toward downtown. Past the feed-and-seed, down East Main Street to the True Value hardware, then left at the pimento cheese factory and over to the old Victorian house once occupied by the owner of the textile mill. Past the new florist and the dental office and the Exxon station on Confederate Avenue, then behind the bottling company and the former library building that had been renovated into a CPA's office. Spent, I rested on the wide, marble steps of the First Baptist Church. I didn't think I'd be accused of trying to score anything illegal there. My running from a high-crime area to a house of worship was unintentional, I think. I'd walked by these same steps a thousand times in daylight hours and never once thought of sitting on them.

My hands were freezing. I cupped them over my mouth and blew. I knew that the future of my marriage might not be up to me. What if, when I returned home, Emily said she'd had enough and was leaving? She could be packing her bags right now while I was touring the town. When I got back, I might find a goodbye note on the door.

Then something awakened in me, and I left the church steps and settled into a brisk walk. I quickened my pace. Once back in my neighborhood, I started walking down the middle of streets instead of on the uneven sidewalks. I remembered tripping on the bricks at that restaurant on my first date with Emily, an inauspicious beginning. And now what of the ending?

I took a left onto Glendale Drive, walking on the streetlight shadows of houses. I jogged up the final hill to Brookside Lane, my lungs aching from the cold air. I had sobered up.

Looking at our darkened house, I imagined Emily asleep, curled up in the fetal position, facing my side of the bed. I was glad when I saw her car in the driveway. She hadn't fled. The door was unlocked. I turned on the den light, waking up the dogs. I nervously walked upstairs to our bedroom. I opened the door slowly, but the old hinge squeaked. It took several seconds for my eyes to adjust. I made out her outline under the covers. She was sleeping in the exact position I'd envisioned.

I came back downstairs and filled up the dogs' water bowls, then got myself some. Glancing at the liquor cabinet, I thought about a drink. Instead, to calm myself I went on the terrace for a smoke, letting the dogs out behind me. Thick clouds were moving in from the east.

I showered in the downstairs guest bathroom so I wouldn't wake Emily. Then I tiptoed up to our bathroom where I brushed my teeth, which for some reason always stimulated mental activity. It was not un-common for me to come up with entire opening arguments for trials when I was brushing in the mornings. I casually surveyed Emily's bric-a-brac—lavender skin lotion, almond shampoo, conditioner with a fusion of mandarin balm and pearls. Could all of this be for another man?

I returned to our bedroom and slipped beneath covers cool at the bed's edge. Emily groaned, rolled over, and warmed me. The curve of her smooth hips was unchanged since the day we'd first met. I held her in my arms and hated myself.

Chapter 18

Six days after my discovery of Emily's emails, I went to the farm. It was a chilly Saturday afternoon. I had just finished working out Midnight. Steam flowed from his nostrils. I was walking around with my yellow Lab, Chief, when a red Chevy pickup came barreling down the barn road. Chief and I both stepped off the gravel because of the driver's reckless speed. The truck got closer, the bearded driver someone I didn't recognize. Staring straight ahead, he flew past me without acknowledgment and ended up having to turn around by the barn. It was possible that he was lost. People occasionally mistook my barn access for a secondary road nearby.

I was glad the horses were in the paddock. The driver negotiated a quick three-point turn, came back toward me, and slammed on his brakes. As he rolled down the passenger side window, I saw that he was alone. I leaned my head in. Mad as I was, it became immediately apparent that his anger far exceeded mine. His face was contorted—jaw clenched, eyes squinting. Probably in his fifties, he was burly, with a pug nose, thick neck, and very hairy fingers. He began furiously scratching at his closely cropped salt-and-pepper beard

"What the *fuck* are you doing, Gil?" he said menacingly.

I said nothing as he stabbed his finger inches from my face. Then he said, "Who the hell you think you're fuckin' with? *Huh?* You're fixing to find out, asshole."

"You've got the wrong address, buddy. There's nobody named Gil living here. If you don't leave now, I'm calling the cops."

He slammed the gear shift into park, got out with the motor running, and quickly walked around the front of his truck toward me. I didn't see any weapons in his hands, nothing around the belt. I backed up a few yards, not knowing what to expect. He was taller than I thought, a good six feet. I hoped I didn't look as scared as I was. Lawyers don't normally have to deal with this kind of nonsense firsthand.

He didn't take a swing at me, but he got right in my face and started poking my chest repeatedly with his finger.

"*You* ain't calling the shots now, motherfucker," he said, spitting out the *f*.

"This is a terrible mistake. I have no idea what you're talking about," I said shakily.

"Talk about mistakes. You think you're the cock of the walk, *don't* ya, Gil? Hot shit from New York. Well, I promise you this: You mess with her again and I'll *kill* you."

Then he backed away slowly so he wouldn't have to turn his back on me. He paused and looked around the property for a few seconds, finally gazing up the hill toward the house.

"Nice place you got here. Be a shame for anything to happen to it."

As he walked back around the truck, I noticed his empty gun rack. Once he sat down, he yelled out the window, "You wanna know what it *feels* like to lose something? *Do ya?* Huh? You *really* wanna know?" I was silent.

He gunned his truck, spraying gravel so far that I had to move back. Then he swerved off the road, running over Chief with his right front tire.

As he passed the gate, he yelled something out his window, but I wasn't paying attention to what he said. My first instinct was to run to Chief, then I quickly realized I would need the truck. I drove over beside where he lay on his side, panting loudly. I felt his high heart rate. His neck was rigid. There was not much blood, just a few minor cuts and scrapes where he'd been rolled, but his back left leg was pointing at a brutal angle, a white tip of bone protruding through the skin. I opened the passenger side door and slid the seat back as far as it would go. When I started to pick him up, he yelped in pain. He had damage to the ribs and I feared his lungs were filling with blood.

I ran to the tack room, grabbed an old blanket that Chief sometimes slept on, and spread it out beside him. Sliding only his haunches and head, I managed to shimmy him onto the blanket. I gathered the edges of the blanket and twisted them tightly around both hands, lifting the makeshift sling and placing it carefully onto the floorboard.

After stopping to lock the gate so the horses couldn't get loose, I got up to 80 on the gravel road, fishtailing on the final curve. I began talking to Chief: *Hold what you got, buddy, hold what you got. We're on the way.* I called my vet Natalie to make sure she was still at the clinic four miles away.

"Chief got hit by a pickup truck. Just now. His ribs are bad, Doc. I'll need a soft stretcher if you have one."

"Yeah. Come to the back door, Jack."

I was a half-mile from Natalie's, waiting impatiently at a stoplight behind two cars, when Chief started coughing up blood. I turned on my flashers and straddled the roadside ditch to get around them. On the highway into town, I flew past a kid driving a souped-up Mustang, hoping there were no cops around. Instead of waiting on two potentially long stoplights ahead, I cut behind the grocery store by the shipping and receiving bays, went up on the curb to get around the locked gates, and came out on Sloan Street.

I started honking my horn as soon as I turned into the parking lot of the clinic. Natalie's assistant Paul was waiting for me at the back door with the stretcher. *We're here, buddy. Hold on. Just hold on.* Natalie came outside with a syringe and gave Chief some painkiller while he was still in the truck. After Paul and I lifted him down onto the stretcher, his coughing got worse.

In the examining room, Natalie gave Chief another shot. She used her stethoscope and then briefly looked inside Chief's mouth. As he groaned deeply, she carefully felt all over his body with both of her hands.

"Accelerated heart rate. Multiple rib fractures. Massive chest trauma." Paul wrote it down.

Natalie ran her hand over the little bumps that had formed on his chest. I softly touched them.

"His lungs are leaking badly. This is irreversible damage, Jack. I'm sorry. There's nothing I can do."

When I got in my truck to leave, I saw that Paul had put Chief's blanket in a plastic bag, untied, and laid it on the front seat. As I rode along with my windows down, oblivious to the cold, tufts of Chief's hair blew around the cab. My passenger seat was indented from where he always sat, attentively taking in the world as it sped by, only barking when he saw other dogs in cars. Two bags of his dry food were in the backseat. I'd been too lazy to carry them inside the night before.

I pulled into the parking lot of a strip mall and cried, my forehead resting on the steering wheel.

I called Gil at the farm and had to leave a voicemail. He was hard to get because he didn't have a cellphone. When he finally called me back hours later, I spoke in a dispirited monotone.

"Does Regina's husband have a red truck?" I asked.

"One of many."

"Is he stocky with a salt-and-pepper beard?"

"Yeah, why?"

Gil kept saying "It's my fault." I didn't argue with him. He spoke slowly, apologizing over and over again. But then he paused. "That piece of *shit!* That fucking *lowlife!*" he suddenly yelled. Had Gil really thought retaliation wasn't headed his way?

"Are you going to do anything about it legally?" he asked.

"Not sure yet. I'm considering it."

"What's there to think about?"

"I'll need a positive ID for one thing."

"Did you get the license plate?"

"It happened too fast. I'll deal with it tomorrow. I'm tired now, Gil."

"Tell me what you want me to do, Jack. You name it and it's done. I'll fuck up this guy's whole world."

"I think you already have. That's the point."

Then I said goodnight. I didn't have it in me to lecture any more. It never worked anyway.

I remembered something important and called him right back.

"FYI, I'm not going to tell Emily her dog was killed on purpose by your girlfriend's husband. That's too complicated for right now. I'll make up a story."

"That's a good idea. I agree with you."

"I'm sure."

Every day the next week, Gil called to see how I was doing. I was busy at work and usually let the calls go to voicemail. "Just checking on you, buddy" was his standard line. I wondered if Gil had truly come to terms with what he'd caused, if he was in fact capable of experiencing real guilt. I was sure his desire for revenge would have him quickly bypassing remorse and moving right on to the nuts and bolts of further fucking up Eric Crowder's life. And anyone else's on the periphery.

Chapter 19

Shit always happens on Saturdays. Too much idle time.

I heard a car coming in the driveway, a sound to which I'd recently become hyperattentive. Through the window, I saw Gil drive up and then run to our side door, accompanied by the usual chorus of barking dogs. He entered without knocking. I could hear him talking with Emily but wasn't able to make out any words. I felt like locking the damn door to my study.

Their conversation was briefer than I expected. I heard the thump and slap of Gil's boots as he walked quickly down the hall toward me. It is dangerously empowering for a certain type of man to start wearing cowboy boots. It's like getting a gun for the first time.

Gil opened the door to the study, again without knocking, and immediately said, "Let's *go*. I know where he is."

"Close the door. Lower your voice."

"I saw his truck at the Lakeside Bar. We can be there in twenty minutes."

I had no interest in going to a bar for a confrontation. Besides, what did he need me for?

"Slow down," I stalled. "Haven't we got time for a beer? The movie's almost over." I pointed unconvincingly to a commercial for Bridgestone tires.

Gil picked up the remote and turned off the T.V. He walked around to the front of my desk, placed his hands on the corners and bent forward so we were at eye level. His still-powerful shoulders and arms flexed as if he were attempting to push my desk through the floor.

"Listen to me, Jackson. If we don't go *right now*, he could be gone when we get there." He flicked his head toward the driveway and then stood upright. If there was anything I'd learned recently, it was that a long-term relationship can come to a crossroads in an instant. Our decades together suddenly felt like a mere prelude to the split-second decision before me.

"So what's the plan when we get there?" I asked.

"Fuck a plan. We'll figure it out when we arrive."

Emily suddenly walked into the study.

"You know where *who* is, Gil?"

"A friend of mine from school."

"Why don't I believe you?"

"Years of knowing me, I guess." He put his hand on Emily's shoulder affectionately, as if consoling someone at a funeral.

"I'll be in the car, Jack," he said from the hallway.

Emily waited until she heard the door close behind him, then said, "Please *God* tell me this isn't about his stupid affair."

"It's got nothing to do with you, Em."

"I can't believe you're getting wrapped up in this nonsense."

"He's going with or without me. You know that."

"So let him go alone. He's a big boy."

"I'm just watching his back, that's all."

Not looking at her, I put my wallet in my jeans and grabbed my coat. I walked to the hall. She followed close behind.

As I went out the door, she yelled: "*You don't owe him anything!*" I kept walking toward Gil's car. He had the radio on full blast and hadn't heard her. Or acted like he hadn't.

I got in and immediately turned off the radio. He pulled out of our drive.

"I can't think with that noise on. I'm not asking for a plan. But at least tell me what the hell you're hoping to accomplish there."

"You'll get a positive ID of Crowder for one thing. Then you can decide if you want to get a warrant for what he did to Chief."

"Don't you think he'll have some friends with him?"

"Crowder is a loner. I think the odds are pretty good he's by himself."

"I can't believe you got Chief killed by this goddamn loser."

Gil glared at me. His right front wheel dipped onto the grass. He overcompensated and pulled back into the middle of the oncoming lane.

"You need to slow down!" I said. "Have you been drinking?"

"Not a drop, Jackson." He cleared his throat loudly, as if to make a point. "I have an idea. Why don't we work together here? I said I was *fucking sorry!* What more do you want? Would you feel better if I paid you a fee for making an appearance today?"

He adjusted the rearview mirror and sped up.

"I'm here, dammit, even though I'll probably be divorced when I get back home."

"Em's not going anywhere. I wouldn't worry about that."

"Don't be too sure."

"Regina's going to leave Eric this time. She's done, Jack. Regardless of the consequences. Chief sealed it."

Gil seemed lost in his thoughts. He continued to drive too fast and cut the curves on the secondary road that leads to the lake. Once he crossed the bridge near the dam and passed by the run-down bait and tackle shops, he took a gravel shortcut that ends up at the back entrance of the Lakeside. He still knew his way around these parts, because nothing here ever changes.

Gil said, "All right, listen. I'll go up and talk to him."

"Are you going to tell him who you are if he still doesn't know?"

"Absolutely. I can't have him thinking you're me."

"What the hell are you going to say to him?"

"I'll play it by ear. There's no use having a prepared speech when someone's coming at you with a broken bottle."

"You really think it'll come to that?"

He began to talk louder, then to shout. "He issued a challenge and I'm letting him know I accept it. I'm going to rearrange his *mother-fucking face.* I've got no choice."

There were a thousand things I could've said but instead I stared out the window silently, letting Gil drive toward our destination like a storm chaser.

The Lakeside is a restaurant/bar with a large outdoor deck. In the spring and summer months, its marina is filled with boaters, fishermen, and drinkers of every stripe. In winter, it becomes a sports bar.

As we slowed to turn in, Gil identified a black Ram truck as Eric's. I reminded him that Chief's killer was in a red Chevy.

"They've got several. I know the truck, *okay*," he said with increasing irritation.

"How do you know she's not with him?" I asked.

"She doesn't like this place. This is his spot."

I started to light a cigarette and Gil stopped me.

"You might need that right hand."

Chapter 20

Fleet and I were seated on the outer edge of our group at the dining table. We were remembering that, as kids, we had both enjoyed watching the *Rockford Files* with our fathers. From the far end of our table, one of the young Skinheads started taunting Fleet: "You ain't got much goin', do ya, boy? I mean, bein' a nigga *and* a cripple. Pretty shitty life."

Lars, Torch, and Ed were engaged in a conversation and didn't hear any of this. Fleet acted like he was ignoring it, but said to me, "What you think Rockford do 'bout this shit?"

I quickly tired of listening to it and told the punk to shut up.

Six Skins started making loud hissing sounds like snakes. Then, they began yelling "Snitch! Snitch! Snitch!" Their voices got louder and louder. They pounded on the table.

Inmates at other tables stared.

Fleet gave the Skins the middle finger. They kept on yelling.

The Firm looked at me. "Brain-dead motherfuckers," Torch said.

Ed rubbed his chin uneasily.

Lesson #4: Don't become the center of attention.

§

Bad news. I found out that Miguel has cancelled his visit tomorrow. I'm not sure what I'm going to do. Will he reschedule? When I saw Ditto and asked him about Miguel, he said, "How the fuck should I know?" The kid's learning curve is a straight line to infinity. If there's a riot in here, he'll be the first to go.

I'll have to see what I can find out from Hawk or Troll. I hope nothing's wrong. Miguel never misses a day. He was planning on discussing St. Paul's conversion on the road to Damascus, one of his favorite stories. I had mischievously planned on telling him about the "conversions" of three preachers and a priest whom I'd represented on charges of criminal sexual conduct with a minor.

§

On Fridays, as our unit arrives on the yard, we get a glimpse into the future. Twenty yards away across a fence line, we see the elderly guys from Unit 5 filing slowly back inside. These are the lifers who are too old and infirm to live around the violent young bucks. One passed away a few months back, so now there are only seven of them. Ed calls Unit 5 the "Hospice Hotel." To a man, they are frail, ashen, downcast. The one known as Debo has deep lines in a face that is a road map of pain.

No one from our unit taunts or insults these men. We wave cordially, as if to grandfathers. It is not so much out of respect as recognition. Occasionally Morris, the one with a walker, will yell over to us, asking if anybody wants to suck his dick. Everyone enthusiastically raises his hand. Morris always gets a kick out of this running gag. Maybe he'll live longer because of it.

"Tired old fools," Booker says with disdain. "Shoot my ass 'fore I get like that."

When he turned seventy a few years ago, the administrators at Congaree arranged to transfer Booker to Unit 5 per DOC regulations. But he was adamant about not wanting to go and enlisted the services of a young pro bono attorney to fight the transfer. The DOC's lawyers assured Booker that he could remain a trusty while he was in Unit 5, but that wasn't his point. "I'd be like a nightwatchman at the graveyard!" he told them. In order to remain in Unit 4, Booker had to sign a stack of waivers a foot high.

And so he takes his chances here. The prisoners don't mess with him. If they did, Torch would crush their skulls. Booker grudgingly steers clear of the Skins, muttering the whole time.

"Didn't use to be so many them motherfuckers."

§

I contemplate the perils, past and present, of eavesdropping.

While sweeping in the rec room, I overheard two young black inmates talking about me.

"Man over there kilt some dude over a *fuckin' dog*."

"You shittin' me."

"He a *lawyer* too."

"*Dumbass*."

This from a man who killed someone over an ounce of crack.

Shortly after Emily found out she couldn't have children, we visited her parents in Charleston for the weekend. I had awakened earlier than usual on Saturday morning and was headed down the carpeted stairway barefooted to get some coffee when I overheard Emily and her mother, Sophie, talking in the kitchen. I stopped after my name was mentioned. I snuck down a few more steps to be closer.

"It could be for the best, sweetie. Depression's in the genes. Jack will come around about adoption. We'll work on him," Sophie said.

"Please don't do that, mother. It comes across as *so* overbearing. Jack doesn't respond to that type of thing. I think his mind's made up, but you and Dad need to stay out of it. *Please*. I mean it."

It was briefly quiet, the only sound the repositioning of a coffee cup. I worried they had heard me, but then Emily asked Sophie if some Charleston news was true. I quietly tiptoed back upstairs.

I never mentioned this episode to Emily. She was successful in preventing her parents from discussing adoption with me. The conversation did color my opinion of Sophie, which wasn't high before that day, even though what she said was true.

§

The word just came down that Easy Ed gets to leave Congaree tomorrow, though under sad circumstances. His father died and, pursuant to a new law, Ed gets to attend the graveside service down in Macon, accompanied by two cops. A day trip, watching the outside world from a moving cell. "Everybody'll be staring," he predicted, "but my momma has me a pinstripe suit to wear. Every chance she gets, she still tells people I'm a good boy."

In the past, the word that Ed has most often used to describe his dad is "evil." A miserable, frustrated high school biology teacher, Ed's father took his anger out on his wife and son with constant verbal abuse. In his rages, he would often grab a glass jar containing a fetus preserved in formaldehyde (one of his classroom exhibits), shove it into young Ed's face, and say, "*This*! This is what we *should've* done with you!" When his parents finally divorced, Ed was a freshman in college. He dropped out to help his mom, got a good-paying job at a local paper mill, and never went back to school. By far the smartest man in Unit 4, Ed reads faster than any lawyer I know. Sometimes when I watch him studiously turning the pages of a book on aeronautics, I can't believe he's in here.

Ed killed his brother-in-law in an alcohol-fueled argument one Christmas Eve. He remains philosophical about his current address: "I knew from my old man that the bottle was no good, but I wasn't strong enough to break the family curse. Liquor and guns: bad combo. When I found out my sister's husband had slapped her around again, I paid him a visit. He laughed about beating her up. Click, that was it. I think I was really killing my dad. I don't need a shrink to tell me that. He's the one who deserved to be shot, not Larry. Larry just needed his ass beat."

Ed's sister Gail eventually forgave him for killing Larry once she got married again. By all accounts, her new husband is kind to her. "So it all worked out good for Gail," Ed said.

When I asked him about what he expected at the funeral, Ed shook his head. "No idea," he said. "I just hope there's no hole waiting for me in that red clay."

Skunk is pissed off about Ed attending the graveside because he didn't get to go to his own mother's funeral recently. He's using me as a sounding board to bitch about the inequity of the situation, like I can do anything about it. I've explained to him that the decision to allow an inmate to attend a parental funeral is entirely discretionary with the DOC and depends upon whether they consider someone a security risk. Skunk is constantly in trouble for fighting and drug possession. He rarely takes his anger management meds, and the crank makes him even more belligerent. He consistently goes to the hole every few months, a poster child for recidivism.

In the most consoling voice possible, I said, "It's prison, Duane. They can do whatever they want. They help people who don't get into trouble and hurt those who do. Ed's record is spotless, you know that. Don't blame him. It's not his fault."

Skunk wasn't at all satisfied with my thoughts on the matter, so I suggested he talk with Miguel.

Still indignant, eyes glassed over, Skunk shouted out, "It ain't right! Ed hated his old man and *he* gets to go! *I fuckin' loved my momma!*"

§

During my nap today, I dreamed I killed Douglas Gunderson. It was an exact re-creation of what happened with Eric Crowder—he was unconscious, I used a tire tool, I hit him three times. Everything was the same, except Eric's face was Douglas's. I didn't seem to be concerned at all about destroying him.

The dream felt like it had been a long time coming, a wave finally reaching shore.

§

When you're in prison, you can't help but think "what if?" It's what the fuck you do all day. I once heard Booker tell a new, young inmate that "them 'what ifs' will eat yo ass up, boy. You best keep 'em quiet."

§

Congaree's okra is tasteless and looks like horse snot. Panic loves it. He always asks for mine and Ed's, which we're happy to give him. To watch and listen to Panic smack his food is to understand why his marriage failed. According to him, when his wife Tonya left and took his son, Cody, she told him that there wasn't another man, the sex was fine, he made enough money, and she liked their house. After that reassurance, Panic's life took a nosedive. He started hanging around with the wrong crowd, i.e., bank robbers. It's unclear why he felt this was a solution to his problems. He had a good job as a welder.

If Panic's dad hadn't killed his mom, maybe she would've taught him the proper table manners that he never learned in the orphanage. And maybe then Tonya wouldn't have bolted. Life's all domino effect.

Countless times, Easy Ed has politely asked Panic to stop smacking, but that just makes him do it louder. He thinks it's funny to be annoying. Given his past, I guess he's entitled to be unrepentant about the little things. I feel bad for letting it get on my nerves, primarily because Panic is diligently searching for a shiv for me. He says he's got a "good lead" on one. I just wish he'd hurry up.

§

Miguel was right. I enjoy literacy instruction and find it rewarding. But it is also tiring. Teaching someone how to read is complicated, with progress individualized. English is a fucking nightmare of rules, exceptions to rules, and idioms. Students need persistence to learn; a teacher needs patience to instruct.

Currently, I have three students and spend four hours a week with each. I have two Hispanics (Carlos and Jose, referrals from Miguel, both speak fairly good English, thankfully) and a white guy named Cliff Campbell. Under the guidelines set forth by the NAAL (National Assessment of Adult Literacy) training materials, I have rated the reading levels of all three as "Below Basic."

Carlos is my slowest learner yet the most optimistic and effusive student, occasionally giving me a high five when he accomplishes something difficult. Jose remains inscrutable throughout our sessions. Cliff is the most impatient, and way too hard on himself. A minor mistake causes him to cuss out of red-faced frustration, although he can laugh at himself shortly thereafter. At 57, he is trying to make up for lost time.

I never would've guessed Cliff couldn't read. I'd spent some time around him before the classes and he was always well-spoken and quick-witted. I find his story compelling. He grew up in the country on his grandfather's livestock farm, working rather than going to school. "There was no DSS around back then," he said. After his grandfather passed, Cliff married a girl from town who got him a job in shipping and receiving with her employer, a trucking company. He was able to keep his illiteracy a secret from his co-workers for decades thanks to his wife reading the invoices for him. The biggest regret of his life (even more so than killing a man over a property dispute) was not being able to read nursery rhymes to his young daughter when she'd begged him to. He said he felt helpless. I look forward to helping him because he's so appreciative. His daughter still visits him regularly along with his wife.

Miguel said that the feedback about my classes is positive. Some other men have already signed up and I'll have to decide if I want to take on any more students.

§

Everything regarding the literacy program is coordinated by Miguel after being cleared by prison administration at Congaree. All I have to do is show up prepared for class.

Reluctantly, I'd agreed to add one more student, hoping not to be overworked. I didn't think twice about not recognizing the name of my newest student, Aaron Langley, since so many folks go by their nicknames. And I also didn't bother finding out who he was before our first meeting. One question to Easy Ed was all it would've taken. It was an inexcusable lapse.

Beef had already brought me to the conference room where, seated, I was spreading out my teaching materials on the desk. I was curious about the identity of my new student. Because I'm mired in the strictest of routines for the better part of my days, I welcomed the element of surprise.

On the other side of the door, I heard Ditto talking and jangling his keys. Aaron's voice was muffled and I couldn't make out what he said. As the heavy door slowly opened, I saw that he was a young white guy who hangs out with the Skins. He's nicknamed Brick because he can't swim. I remembered him from the aftermath of the ping pong incident, talking a lot of shit and making threats as he walked away down the corridor.

Brick was outraged, as if he'd been tricked into being there. He said angrily, "*Oh hell fuckin' no. I ain't doin' it.*" This outburst seemed to be addressed to the guards more than me. Brick was twenty feet away from me and double-cuffed, so I wasn't worried about him trying to come at me.

He looked directly at Ditto and said, "We're *done* here. Take my ass back to the cell."

"You ain't in charge, fuckface," Ditto said. "My instructions was to bring you here for two hours."

"It's okay," Beef said to Ditto. "You can take him back. The class is called off for today. Right, Counselor?"

"Seems so."

"What a goddamn waste of my time," Ditto said. "I got paperwork I coulda been doing."

"Listen," Beef said, "in the future, these two inmates should never be together. Put that in your paperwork. I'll check behind you to make sure. Y'all go on now."

Brick glared at me and said, "Fuck ya later, *snitch*."

Beef calmly said, "Son, you're awfully cocky for someone who can't even read God's word. You need to humble yourself and quit hanging around those Nazis." He then pointed at Brick. "If anything happens to Counselor here, you're going to the hole whether you did it or not. Now get outta here."

Brick said, "We're taking over this place, old man, and there's nothin' you can fuckin' do about it. We *are* God."

With a surprisingly quick motion, Beef grabbed his billy stick and kneecapped Brick. It wasn't hard enough to break anything, but Brick will be limping for a few days. As he fell to the floor screaming "motherfucker" multiple times, I casually gathered up my instructional materials. I'd never seen Beef lose his cool before. He has strong convictions.

Ditto looked down at Brick and said, "You don't much look like God."

"Shut up, Corporal," Beef said. "This ain't funny. Once that prisoner can get off the floor, take him back to his cell immediately. And no rough stuff on the way."

"Yes sir. But what if he needs a wheelchair?" Ditto asked.

"No wheelchair. He can walk or he can crawl."

Brick was still in the fetal position, moaning. Lesson #5: Know your place.

As Beef and I walked back to my cell through the long, desolate corridors of Congaree, we stopped every now and then for him to take a breather. I worry about his heart. That's a lot of weight to carry around. He voiced his concerns about an upcoming physical, mentioning that he's still three years away from state retirement. If he gets forced out of here for health reasons, he'll be working the cash register at his brother-in-law's convenience store.

Right before we entered my cell block, Beef said, "Sorry you had to see that, Jack." He looked at me, a convicted murderer, hoping to see something like forgiveness.

"I understand," I said. And I do.

During a restless night, I wondered whether or not Aaron Langley would one day learn to read. If he does, the first thing the Skins will give him is some white supremacist propaganda to reinforce his views, so maybe I am wrong to hope he finds another teacher. It's probably best that he remains illiterate; otherwise, he'll be able to enlist more recruits, be better prepared to pass on the poison.

Chapter 21

We went through a stage, early in our marriage, when we enjoyed entertaining friends at dinner parties. There wasn't much else to do in a small town like Warrington. Emily was a good cook and knew a fair amount about wine. After a glass or two, still wearing her chef's apron, she liked to regale our guests with a favorite story about how I subjected her to rigorous cross-examination when we started dating.

"He starts bombarding me with a ton of questions right and left. The real third degree. In that *serious tone*. It's like I'm stuck in a damn deposition or something." She imitated me with a deep register. "You are a dog lover, I presume? Good, because that's a non-negotiable condition, regardless of my affection for you. Hey, when I'm out of town, you wouldn't mind feeding five dogs every morning before you go to work, would you? *What?* You're *scared* of horses? Ooooh, that's a major deduction from your overall score, considering I much prefer the company of horses to humans anyway. *Hmm...things aren't looking too good.* Young lady, I'm really not sure if you're going to pass or fail. Perhaps we should move on to the all-important category of music, about which I know more than any other living person. You're kidding me, Emily, you really don't love Dylan and Waits? *It's about the lyrics!* I am quite concerned about your test score at this juncture. I mean, this is liable to be a very close call. Continued bachelorhood is looking awfully appealing to me."

She might take a wine break here. I spent years watching friends laugh at my expense.

"I'm here to tell you, the man was on a mission that night! Hell, I was worried he might try to get into my panties; instead he's giving me a freakin' *compatibility quiz*. He should go to work for one of those computer dating services instead of getting drunks out of DUIs in this one-horse town."

"It's a good thing you're not behind the wheel tonight, Em." I'd retort.

"And then there's his annoying habit of having the last word on everything," she'd say.

Though hugely entertaining, Emily's comedy routine omitted certain vital information. For example, I actually found her musical knowledge to be quite impressive, especially given her youth. She was fortunate that her mother had been a hippie for a few years and retained her extensive album collection, which Emily had made use of while growing up. However, there were glaring deficiencies. Most notably, she was unfamiliar with Van Morrison's "Queen of the Slipstream." I was glad to be of some small service by introducing her to it. She immediately succumbed to the song's charms and we eventually chose it for the spotlight dance at our outdoor wedding along the banks of the Ashley River. At the beginning we slow danced to it, my right hand resting comfortably on the small of her back, and when the pace of the song sped up, we did the foxtrot. We both had taken dancing lessons as kids and that was something we had in common. Not an insignificant thing, the shared enjoyment of dancing.

What she said about my affection for animals was true. It would be nearly impossible for me to coexist with someone who couldn't have a pack of dogs around her at all times. But Emily grew up with a beloved family dachshund named Winston and had missed him desperately when she'd gone up North to school. I knew she was ripe for canine expansion. The fact that all of my dogs were over fifty pounds might've been pushing it, though.

As for horses, despite my best efforts and my commendable patience, Emily could never overcome her fear of sitting atop a twelve-hundred-pound animal in motion. I didn't push the issue because the last thing I wanted was her getting injured trying to please me. There are a thousand ways to get hurt around horses if you don't know what you're doing. In lieu of riding together, she painted large portraits of my horses that we hung in our den.

Thus, a routine evolved between us in which I taught her about popular music and she schooled me in art. Relationships have been built with weaker mortar. It worked for a while.

§

When I practiced law, the wives of my incarcerated clients would occasionally call me. They were distraught, lonely, wanting me to cheer them up, to tell them everything was going to be all right, that the less-than-promising appeal might somehow prevail, that eight years or fifteen years really wasn't *that* long to wait for their husbands to get out. Sometimes they would call late at night, crying, drunk, high, desperate to talk. I always tried to comfort them.

After six months behind bars, I had to decide what to do about Emily. Obviously, my situation was unfair to her on many levels. It created a sense of obligation and put her life on hold.

Emily would eventually find someone, with or without my knowledge. I had no idea how long this would take. She would drift away, need companionship, start seeing someone, probably feel guilty about it. Appeals take years. Even if I were to prevail in the Court of Appeals and get out for a while, the State would certainly take my case up to the Supreme Court, which could put me right back here. Emily had disregarded the advice of her parents and stood by me throughout the humiliation of the trial. As I saw it, she deserved to be rewarded by not having to put up with me anymore.

Talking to someone through the glass is intimate in the sense that you're physically close to each other and it's quiet around you, but not being able to touch Emily was torture. Her hair was right there. So often she'd carelessly brushed it back from her face when laughing or dancing. Yet now, inches away, it was already just memory.

I paused before speaking. "Prisoners don't have many rights. But we do get to choose who's on our visitors' list. No one, not even a spouse, can force their way onto the list. Did you know that? You're the only woman I ever loved," I choked out. "This is goodbye, Em." Her eyes narrowed. The reflection of my contorted face in the glass was strangely frightening.

She started to say something but I interrupted her. Our time was up. It was the right thing to do under the circumstances. She had to hate me.

"It's all my fault. Maybe if I'd agreed to adopt a child things would've been different," I said.

Emily's eyes started blinking rapidly and she bit her bottom lip. I thought she would start crying. Instead she jumped out of her chair and screamed, "*I know what you're doing!*" After a wide backswing, as far as the metal cord would stretch, she slammed the phone receiver against the glass, causing a small, spidery crack.

Her outburst caught the attention of the guards, who came over and quickly escorted her away. Wives who are belligerent don't get to stick around long in Congaree. They upset the inmate and "make him unpredictable," Hawk says. When she was out of sight, I could still hear Emily yelling, "I'm leaving. Get your hands off me. I'm going. Don't you *dare* touch me." There was a mix of fury and resignation in her voice.

Though she often talked tough, this was the first time I'd ever seen her smash anything. And why shouldn't she? I had done the same thing.

I remained seated for a while. I apologized to Beef. He accepted it without questions. Understanding as always, Beef told me he wasn't worried about the crack.

"Why don't you collect yourself, Jack," he said. "We're in no hurry to get back."

I gazed at the crack in the glass, her final piece of artwork for me. It was no more than an inch long. I studied it as if a scientist peering through a microscope. The longer I stared at the crack, the more I convinced myself that it was shaped like the state of Florida, just like the birthmark on Emily's neck.

Her birthmark had taken on great importance during our marriage. Since she was very ticklish on her neck, I got into the habit of initiating foreplay by kissing her birthmark and joking around: "Watch out! I'm going to Florida!" Lounging in bed after lovemaking, I would often gaze at the birthmark, memorizing its exact outline. While she slept, I'd watch that part of her neck gently pulsate as she breathed.

Emily moved to New Mexico the next month.

Chapter 22

Last night I dreamed about my trial: A slow-moving eighty-year-old bailiff walked onto the balcony of the Logan County Courthouse overlooking Beauregard Street and the town square. He rang a handbell and yelled, "Hear ye! Hear ye! Court is now in session. The Honorable Gordon Sumwalt presiding." I could smell azaleas and hear robins chirping. As the bailiff returned and closed the balcony door, it sounded exactly like my cell door clanging shut. I woke up.

April is a cruel month to try a man for murder.

§

At most, I was guilty of voluntary manslaughter. This was a textbook heat-of-passion killing, devoid of premeditation. Sometimes you don't know what you're going to do until you do it. Originally I wanted to tell the truth, to take the blame, and have my lawyer negotiate a plea deal that wasn't the equivalent of life. That way, Gil could plead to something minor like trespassing, thereby avoiding the harsh consequences of my ill-considered action, despite all the incredibly stupid shit he'd done leading up to it. If I made it to my late seventies, I might get to see the farm again. But a plea deal was wishful thinking.

In his first communication with us, the prosecutor made it clear there would be no negotiating. Eric Crowder's angry parents wanted us both to go down, especially Gil, and given the facts of the case, that was the most likely outcome. It didn't matter to the prosecutor which one of us had killed Eric. We both were on Eric Crowder's property, he boasted, and we both would be convicted of murder.

Oftentimes, the criminal justice system forces family members to prove their love for one another in the most sacrificial ways. Because of the facts of our case, the legal theory of accomplice liability ("The hand of one is the hand of all.") forced us, strategically, to have a unified front. In the end, it was a partnership destined for disaster. And this much is certain: Neither of us would be in prison if it weren't for the other one.

§

To this day, I compare all lawyers to Uncle Robert. When I went looking for one of my own, his lofty standard was the model I had in mind. I wanted a local from Logan County, someone a jury would identify with and possibly know. The logical choice became obvious early on. I had briefly socialized with Fred Mobley at statewide Bar functions, where he was a frequent speaker known for his fierce intelligence and sly sense of humor. A decade older than me, he possessed the natural people skills of a populist politician. Fred was streetwise yet well-connected in his community—board of directors for the hospital, president of the arts council, elder in the First Presbyterian Church, member of the Rotary Club. He could play the good ol' boy with the best of 'em, but in a courtroom he was ruthless, and ruthlessness was what I needed.

Fred was a thorough cross-examiner, his brain quickly working through a myriad of possibilities. His asking the right question at the right time often undermined the credibility of witnesses, the impact on jurors sometimes palpable.

The best trial lawyers, such as Fred, are actors and actresses. To win the jury, they must have the common touch—not too silver-tongued to cause distrust, not too fashionable to foster resentment, not too haughty to engender hostility.

Gil's selection of a defense attorney, unfortunately, was foolish. I explained the benefits of choosing a local lawyer whom Fred had recommended, but Gil wouldn't hear of it. A trusted literary friend of his in New York referred him to a prep school friend, Chadwick "Chad" Hollingsworth, from Charleston.

I suspected Gil was getting financial help from Charlie Reese, so paying for a lawyer was not an issue. Gil requested that I look into Hollingsworth. The reviews were lukewarm. At age fifty-six, Chad had a reputation as competent but unexceptional, his long lunches and abbreviated office hours viewed less as laziness than as privilege born of a sizable inheritance. A classmate of Chad's said he was "okay for bullshitting a jury if that's all you want. The problem is Chad doesn't understand evidence law and won't take the time to learn it. He won't know how to preserve the record for appeal."

Still, the most troubling thing I heard was from a lifelong Charlestonian: "Even Chad's fellow SOBs think he's a snob." My fear, later confirmed at trial, was that he would stick out in a rural setting. And he did, especially when he flashed his chartreuse-flecked yellow socks.

Gil went down to Charleston and met with Chad for ninety minutes, then retained him on the spot, despite my objections. Later, as Chad's shortcomings became obvious in court, all I could think about was Uncle Robert, the model of humility and industriousness, being appalled by his son's misguided choice.

The young prosecutor, Ainsley Dunn, was a second-generation solicitor trying to live up to his father's legacy. Most people in Logan County had liked and respected the late "Big Bill" Dunn. At six-foot-six, he was a towering, charismatic, hard-nosed figure who ruled his fiefdom for over thirty years. He prided himself on seeking the death penalty in any case that qualified. Uncle Robert had thought highly of Big Bill and considered him a worthy adversary in court. But we'd heard that locals were still on the fence about "young Dunn." Winning our case would certainly boost his reputation.

Ainsley was smart. He'd gone to Cornell undergrad then come back home to attend law school at the University of South Carolina, knowing he had a job waiting once he passed the bar exam. He was sharp enough to know that everything about Chief's death cut both ways. It provided an obvious motive for the prosecution to exploit but also created a useful defense tool with which to try and finagle a hung jury based on sympathy, or *nullification* as it's known. There's an unwritten law in these parts: Did the person deserve killing? If so, was the defendant someone who had good cause to do it? I'd seen nullification work more than once. Ainsley countered by continually emphasizing the brutality of the assault.

In reviewing the jury list before trial, I knew I had a "ringer" who would hold out for the defense even if isolated by an 11-1 vote. He was a retired, unassuming grandfatherly type with no criminal record whom I believed the State would surely seat. I doubted the prosecution was aware that his two wayward grandsons lived in my county and that I'd saved them from going to jail multiple times on serious drug distribution charges.

During *voir dire*, when the State asked if anyone on the jury panel knew me, he remained quiet. I sensed that I was one step closer to a hung jury at the very least. But the clerk of court never pulled his name out of her rotating box. It was the worst possible luck.

A number of the jurors knew Fred. Three of them said they couldn't be fair and impartial and were excused from service. You always hate to lose those people too. We held our last strike in case the clerk called the name of a guy who was an electrical engineer. I never took engineers; they're skeptical, precise types who think they know everything, just like airline pilots.

We ended up with a jury consisting of two housewives, a welder, an insurance agent (the foreperson), a restaurant owner, a peach farmer, a fifth-grade teacher, a nurse, a college student, a dental hygienist, a power company lineman, and a salesman. Despite the setbacks, I distinctly recall thinking that the jury seemed like a fair-minded group of folks.

Later, the teacher would avert her eyes from the autopsy photos of Eric Crowder's skull fractures, and the college student would be unable to touch the bloody tire iron that was introduced into evidence. The transcript reflects that, over the course of trial, Ainsley Dunn said "blunt force trauma" a total of 16 times and "bludgeoned" 23 times. It was obviously effective.

§

Given the circumstances of our case, Gil and I knew we had to take the stand. There was no other way for our story to fully come out. Prime example: How else would the jury hear about what happened at the Lakeside Bar? This was a crucial part of our defense. We testified that Eric Crowder, when referring to his wife, said he was "going to kill that fucking bitch," after which he hastily exited the bar. Gil saw this comment as an immediate threat, thus our subsequent high-speed chase and presence at the Crowder residence. We hoped this scenario would dovetail nicely with Regina's testimony that Eric had been physically abusive during their marriage.

Even so, I knew that whenever you waive your Fifth Amendment privilege, you're giving a good prosecutor the blueprint for building a bomb.

We were also confronted with what lawyers pragmatically refer to as "unfriendly facts." When a crime is obvious, a fair amount of fictionalizing is required. Having not provided written statements allowed us plenty of flexibility in this regard.

Our story was that *only I* wielded the tire iron. Immediately after Gil was shot, I engaged in a life-or-death struggle with Eric, who had a loaded gun. My hitting him in the head four times was in self-defense.

Since my DNA was found on the gun, it would've been easy enough to say that I'd picked it up after my altercation with Eric, checked to see how many rounds were left (none by then), and dropped it back on the ground. But an empty pistol is not the most threatening thing in the world, at least not to the jurors who were knowledgeable about fire-arms and might be skeptical that a gun enthusiast like Eric didn't realize how many rounds he'd fired, even under duress.

If I hoped to have a viable self-defense argument under the circumstances of "mutual combat," it was critical I testify that Eric's gun was still loaded with one shot at the time of our altercation. Otherwise, Ainsley might stumble upon the truth: I had killed a defenseless man. In any self-defense case, justification is a function of urgency.

During the actual incident, as opposed to our fabricated one, Eric had been facing Gil when Eric was initially hit in the head by the flying tire iron. (It was a remarkably accurate throw by Gil, from twelve yards away, according to the police sketch of the crime scene.) This meant that the injury was in the frontal lobe in the same general vicinity as the blows I administered only moments later. The original wound appeared consistent with the struggle that I related to the jurors.

The truly amazing thing is that our lives came down to a split second: Eric shot Gil at the exact time the tire iron was in flight. If Gil had waited one moment longer to release it, we'd both be dead. To me, it's the most incredible part of our case, and the jury would never even hear about it.

Ainsley spent a lot of time on the specifics of my struggle with Eric, as I assumed he would. He tried his best to get me to contradict my direct testimony in the most minute ways, but he was unsuccessful. Gil and I had rehearsed the scenario many times in preparation for cross-examination. We'd spent hours "blocking out" my imaginary fight, like movie directors considering every conceivable movement and angle.

A trial is a jumble of information that an effective lawyer must shape into a succinct argument for a jury to easily digest, a difficult task. Only a small percentage of lawyers do it well. Chad Hollingsworth did not. Maybe his desultory performance was due to nerves, or maybe he simply was exhausted. Chad wasn't horrible; he just didn't speak with

the requisite conviction. I've seen public defenders argue more passion-
ately about misdemeanors that carry thirty days.

Displaying his usual lack of attention to detail, Chad mistak-
enly referred to Detective Garrett as *Garner* several times. If Fred had
done that, he'd make sure the jury knew it was a purposeful backhanded
swipe. With Chad, it seemed just another mistake.

He performed best during his closing when he navigated the
tricky terrain that distinguishes co-defendants. He had to separate his
client from me in case the jury didn't want to entertain a package deal:
"Don't forget, ladies and gentlemen of the jury, my client is the person
who got shot, and he was *not* the one who used the tire iron. I urge you
to disregard what the Solicitor said about accomplice liability because
there was absolutely no plan between these two defendants. That we can
be sure of. Once Eric Crowder threatened his wife at the bar, this whole
thing was by the seat of the pants. The hand of one is not the hand of all
when neither hand knows what the other's doing." This made more sense
than anything Chad had said all week.

Afterward, Gil slipped me a note saying *I didn't tell him to say
that shit,* which I truly considered a thoughtful gesture.

Chad's comments were merely the equivalent of my lawyer emphasizing that I was not driving the car during the chase and I was not
the one romantically involved with Regina, both necessary legal arguments.

§

Ainsley argued that the week between Chief's death and the
incident constituted a "waiting period" under the law, during which time
Gil and I assiduously planned Eric's murder:

"I ask you to pay very close attention to the timing of events
leading up to Eric Crowder's death. Look at when his wife went out of
town to Florida, and then look at when these defendants chose to strike

against her husband. They were lying in wait for him. They even chased him down on his *own property* in order to kill him. And make no mistake, under the law known as the Castle Doctrine, 'a man's home is his castle,' and you better *believe* Mr. Crowder had every right to shoot at these intruders in self-defense."

Walking metronomically in front of the jury, he concluded with "One of these defendants slept with Mr. Crowder's wife and then they both conspired to murder him. Is it possible to do worse to another person?"

Truth be told, it wasn't a difficult case to prosecute. I feared that the jury sensed Ainsley's earnestness, which is always bad for the opposition.

Ainsley and Gil sparred on cross. At times it seemed like a battle of educational pedigree—the upstart Ivy Leaguer versus the old-style Vandy man. The jury seemed to enjoy the intense sniping, but I don't think it did Gil any good to square off with Ainsley. I suspect Gil underestimated him, with his spindly build and measured strides. Prior to taking the stand, a confident Gil had co-opted Hemingway's famous dig at T. S. Eliot, saying, "That kid's never hit a ball out of the infield, Jack."

"Not yet," I warned.

Ainsley was intent on giving Gil additional motive.

"Where did you say you met Mrs. Crowder the first time?"

"The answer is still the same, the Tractor Supply store outside Warrington. The one by the Interstate."

"Was this a chance meeting or by design?"

"Entirely coincidental, of course."

"What were you doing there?"

"Buying horse feed and some other supplies. I was helping my cousin look after his horses."

"So you didn't know who Regina Crowder was before then?"

"No. How could I?"

"Did you start up a conversation with her?"

"Yes."

"Why?"

"Have you not seen her?"

"Is that the only reason you have for talking to a woman, that's she's physically attractive?"

"No, sir. Intelligence and humor are also traits I admire. I'll freely admit I enjoy the company of women, Mr. Dunn, if that's what you're getting at."

"Or did you talk to her because you knew she was wealthy, or that her husband was?"

"How on earth would I know that?"

"It's a small community. People talk. Regina Crowder was a nice catch for you, wasn't she, Mr. Hampton? It's not like you were on the bestseller list."

"Are you serious?"

"Entirely."

Gil smirked, then said, "Look, I know this may come as a surprise to you, but not everyone is a cad. Believe it or not, people do still fall in love."

"Indeed, Mr. Crowder being one. I understand you just recently moved back down South several months before this incident took place. Is that correct, Mr. Hampton?"

"Yes, I'd say about five months beforehand."

"And how long had you lived in New York City?"

"Almost thirty years."

"Why did you move back to Warrington after all this time?"

"New York's gotten too expensive. And I had abandoned a writing project that I was dissatisfied with and thought I might be inspired by coming home. You always hope that a change of geography will somehow stimulate you."

"Did you have writer's block?"

"No, I was writing. I just didn't like what I was writing."

"Would you describe yourself as a frustrated artist?"

"No. I've been published, so I achieved my dream. I never expected to get rich doing what I do."

"So you were strapped financially?"

"I have some savings. Nothing you'd call substantial. The cost of living up there makes it hard to get ahead."

"Being with Regina Crowder would solve your cash flow problem, though, wouldn't it?"

"There you go again, trying to mislead this jury. Let me be clear: This was not about money. I'm no *gold digger*, and I resent the implication."

"I'm curious, did sleeping with a younger, wealthier, married woman recharge your creative batteries, Mr. Hampton?"

"Being with someone I care for did, yes. The rest didn't matter."

"So it didn't matter to you that she was married?"

"Certainly it did. That was something we were going to have to deal with in the future."

"And you dealt with it by planning to kill her husband, didn't you?"

"That's untrue. It's a fiction that you and Detective Garrett have created."

"And the fact that Eric killed your cousin's dog made it that much easier, didn't it?"

"Wrong again. Think about it: Why would I go to all that trouble when Regina could just divorce him? Why is this so hard for you to comprehend, Mr. Dunn?"

Judge Sumwalt intervened, saying, "Mr. Hampton, just answer the questions, don't editorialize. Let your lawyer make the arguments."

Ainsley continued:"But Regina wouldn't come out nearly as good financially with a divorce as she would if Eric died."

"I didn't know the first thing about Crowder's finances."

"You testified earlier that you had seen the Crowder residence from the road. Eric's wealth was evident."

"I couldn't care less. I was interested in his wife, not his money."

As an attorney, I knew the cross was not going well for Gil. Every time Ainsley scored a point, Gil's arrogance appeared to increase exponentially.

§

Over the years I'd seen women go to extraordinary lengths to help Gil, and Regina Crowder was no exception. She held up well under Ainsley's examination, as Gil had promised she would. As much as I sometimes want to, I can't blame her for my conviction.

Regina's in-laws blamed her for what happened to their son. They tried to pressure the prosecution into charging her with conspiracy to commit murder, but there was no evidence for such a charge. It was a classic study in power, with the full force of the Crowder's family fortune being brought to bear. My investigator Ron Patton put it succinctly: "It's easier to get away with killing a poor man than a rich one." Ron reported that Eric's parents, now in their late seventies, along with their personal attorney from Atlanta had visited the Solicitor's office six times in the weeks leading up to trial. Even though Eric hadn't lived in Logan County very long, he was one of its wealthiest citizens and had given generously to many worthy causes. Ron said Eric's father wanted the death penalty. The old man was not happy when Ainsley explained that ours was not a capital crime.

As furious as Regina was about the Crowder's attempts to railroad her, she knew there was a later battle to be fought with them in probate court over her inheritance. Eric's estate was conservatively estimated to be worth ten million, and Regina had Eric's will on her side. It had been prepared by the Crowder's family attorney three years prior.

It soon became obvious with Ainsley's questioning of Regina that Inez Crowder was adamant that her son *not* be portrayed as an abusive husband. Strategically, another prosecutor may have handled this a different way, but I got the feeling Ainsley didn't have a choice in the matter. Therefore, he risked alienating the women on the jury by trying to discredit Regina's abuse claims, constantly inquiring about why she never reported her alleged abuse to the police, insisting that she was "in cahoots" with the defense, insinuating that she was trying to keep her lover out of prison. Examining an alleged victim of abuse is always a delicate matter requiring a cautious approach from a lawyer, so we were pleased when Ainsley chose an aggressive strategy.

Regina shed her cowgirl look for court. She had on a black skirt that fell just above the knee, a cream-colored blouse, and low heels. Her long hair was back in a clip, and her pearl necklace was understated. Her conservative appearance seemed appropriate for a widow. The problem was that Regina was almost too beautiful. She looked like the type of woman that men *would* kill for, and I suspect some of the female jurors disliked her for it. Emily had long voiced her concern about this possibility. She knew.

Specificity always enhances a witness's credibility. Regina was at her best when describing the particular details of her abuse. There was a raw honesty to her account that made me glad we hadn't tried to coach her too much.

Recalling the first time she was hit, Regina testified: "I talked to Eric's cousin Tom for a long time over the Christmas holidays and this made him mad. I think Eric had been jealous of him since they were kids. When we got back from the holidays, Eric kept harping on it over and over again. He wouldn't let it go. He kept saying: 'What did y'all talk about? Did Tom try and sleep with you? You like him, don't you?' That kinda thing. When I told Eric he was way off base, he slapped me with the back of his hand, out of the blue, while he was walkin' by on the way to the fridge. I was in shock. He got me right across the cheekbone. You could see the mark from his ring in the swelling. He said he was sorry the next day when he sobered up. Sometimes he'd say he was sorry and sometimes not."

"Do you think he always remembered what happened?" Fred asked.

"Yeah, he knew. He wasn't a blackout drinker. Just a heavy one."

"How many times would you say your husband struck you during the course of your marriage?

"Five times. Three slaps and two hits with his fist."

"You're very specific with that number."

"You don't forget."

"I'm sorry to have to dwell on this, but can you please tell us about a time when Eric used his fist on you?"

"One was when I said I was going to Louisville for a barrel racing competition. Eric didn't want me to go. We argued about it. I said, 'You know this is what I do, right?' Then he polished off a whole bottle of Jack Daniels and it was on. He started throwin' my cowboy boots at the walls, then at me. I got a lot of boots, you know. When I tried to run out the door, he punched me in the eye. That man had a fist like a *rock*. I was dizzy when I got up. It made me cry and that don't happen much.

"A few days later, his mama insisted on coming for a visit. He tried to put her off but Inez gets what she wants. That's when Eric had me tell her that my horse reared its head and hit me. There was no way to cover up a black eye the whole time. I mean, I couldn't wear sunglasses at the supper table."

In his closing, Fred made a big deal about the prosecution getting tough with Regina. His face flush with indignation, Fred said, "Normally they're in the business of *protecting* them, not *persecuting* them! To try to get their case to make any kind of sense, the State has sold its soul to the

Devil. Watching Mr. Dunn attack a victim of domestic violence when he's supposed to be entrusted with helping her is the most disgraceful thing I've seen in a court of law in thirty-five years! Mrs. Crowder was very brave to come in here and tell the truth about the physical abuse she suffered at the hands of her late husband. She has now been mistreated at home and here in court. No *wonder* more women don't come forward in domestic abuse cases."

As Regina left the courtroom, I watched Inez and the rest of the family glare at her, their faces those of an angry mob wanting to stone a woman to death.

§

Fred Mobley's masterful trial advocacy was on full display in a losing cause. "Sometimes in life," he said, "you're faced with a situation where you must decide whether or not to help someone that you believe is in danger. It may come at great personal risk to you, but you know in your heart that it's the right thing to do.

"Eric Crowder lured these two men over to his property. He duped them. This was a set-up from the very beginning, pure and simple. The solicitor talked a lot about revenge. Well, the revenge was on the part of Eric Crowder because his wife had fallen in love with Mr. Hampton. Make no mistake, *that's* the revenge in this case. Eric Crowder knew exactly what he was doing. And he knew just exactly what to say to get these two men—with no prior criminal records whatsoever!—to go onto his property so he could kill them and try to get away with it. Just remember: Mr. Crowder *purposely* left his electric gate wide open so these men could drive right through. One press of a button was all he had to do and he could've kept them out. But no, he let 'em in because he had his gun ready and waiting."

As Fred picked up a heavy law book off our table, he said slowly, "Eric Crowder tricked these men into coming onto his property by threatening to *kill* his wife when he saw them at the Lakeside Bar and Grill. They didn't know he was conning them, that it was a deadly trap. Now listen to this. This is the law regarding defense of others." He put on his glasses, cleared his throat, and read from the book:

"Under the law of self-defense, a defendant may take another's life in the defense of others. The defense of another person is excusable if the defendant had reasonable grounds to believe, and in good faith did believe, that the person being defended was in imminent danger of death or serious bodily harm from the victim. The defendant does not have to show that the person he defended was actually in danger. It is enough if the defendant believed the person was in imminent danger. The defendant has the right to act on appearances even though the defendant's beliefs may have been mistaken. The defendant must show that a reasonably prudent person of ordinary firmness and courage would have had the same belief under the circumstances."

He carefully closed the book and cradled it in his right arm.

"And these men had very good reason to believe that Regina Crowder was in imminent danger because they knew her husband had physically abused her several times in the past. You heard her testimony. Eric had hit her with his fist and slapped her around. So they went to the Crowders' property to help her. *Lawfully.*

"Now imagine the scene there if you're my client and his cousin. This has all been very spur of the moment. Things have happened very quickly. You've come to save Regina Crowder but you have no firearms. You didn't know she wasn't there. You're being shot at by Eric Crowder, who's had his pistol ready and waiting for this very moment. Somehow you have to defend yourself, or you will die. It's an awful position to be in. You do what you have to do in order to survive. And our laws provide for this very situation.

"Think about it: If this had been a *premeditated* murder—something these men had been planning—why in the world would they show up at Mr. Crowder's place without a weapon? And who gets in a car chase in a Subaru? It makes no sense! These are not ignorant men. You heard them on the stand. They believed Regina Crowder was in serious danger. And remember Detective Garrett's testimony. He said the first thing out of my client's mouth was about Mrs. Crowder, and that they had come to help her. Very first thing, that's what Mr. Merritt said."

Fred then described me as "a pillar of the community," juxtaposing my character—spotless record, attorney in good standing—with that of a man who was "a dog killer and a wife beater." In closing, he said, "The State's decision to prosecute this case shows their fundamental misunderstanding of human nature and their inability to tell the good guys from the bad guy. But I'm trusting that you ladies and gentleman of the jury can tell who the good guys are because of your common sense, fairness, and decency."

§

As a practicing lawyer I was nervous many times in a court, once almost fainting when my knees locked up during opening argument of a federal drug trafficking trial. But no amount of courtroom experience can prepare you for what it's like being a murder defendant sitting in the witness chair. Most criminal defense lawyers like to think they can imagine that feeling, but they don't have a clue.

Chomping at the bit on his cross-examination of me, Ainsley said, "Isn't the real reason you didn't report the dog incident to law enforcement was so you could seek your *own* brand of vigilante justice against Mr. Crowder?"

"Without a gun, Mr. Dunn? That wouldn't have been very smart. The best evidence against your argument is that I *didn't* have a gun with me, like my cousin said. I'm sure you don't want to concede this because it hurts your case so much. The reason I..."

"How did you feel when your dog died?"

"Sad."

"Weren't you also angry?"

"Do you know a dog owner who wouldn't be? Do you not have a dog, Mr. Dunn?"

"This is about you, not me. Were you angry, yes or no?"

"Of course I was, but my dog is not the reason I was in Eric Crowder's front yard. I was there to help his wife, who I thought was in danger. I understand you're trying to work your motive angle as a prosecutor, but let me just say that the main reason your version is not true is because I'm *not* a murderer. I could never take another person's life unless it was in self-defense or to protect another person. But the death of my dog *did* make me and my cousin think that Eric could kill his wife. And that's what this whole thing is about."

"So why didn't you attempt to prosecute Eric Crowder if you thought he intentionally ran over your dog?"

"First of all, I wasn't positive who he was at the time. I didn't have an exact identification because I couldn't get his license plate number. Granted, I had a good idea after I talked to Gil, but that's not enough. Plus, I was scared of him. Don't forget he threatened to kill me that day thinking I was my cousin. I didn't know what this man was capable of."

"Are you trying to tell this jury that you, who chased Mr. Crowder for two miles at high speeds and confronted him on his own property, were afraid of *him*."

"That's exactly what I'm saying, Mr. Dunn. And I was even more afraid of him when he started shooting at us."

"You were on his property. Who could blame him?"

"We were unarmed. Can you blame *us* for following him after the threat he made against his wife and knowing what he'd done to my dog?"

"It's one thing to kill a dog and quite another to kill your wife."

"Seems like the same personality type to me. With all due respect, Mr. Dunn, you're not considering the fact that Eric Crowder lured us over there. He didn't close his front gate. He let us in and then ambushed us."

"With all due respect, you and your cousin don't strike me as the type of men who are easily tricked."

"Neither do you, but you've also been totally fooled by Eric's scheme. You don't believe our story and you're trying to prosecute us. He's convinced you too, posthumously. See what I mean? Make no mistake, he knew what he was doing on that day."

Feigning incredulity, Ainsley put his hands on his hips and said, "Mr. Merritt, as a lawyer, are you *really* trying to suggest that your dog's death didn't create a powerful motive?"

"As a prosecutor, are you really trying to say that Regina's adultery didn't create a powerful motive for her husband to kill my cousin and me because I was with him?"

For me, this predictable kind of point/counterpoint only seemed to magnify the absurdity of my situation. It felt like I'd been horribly miscast in a career-defining dramatic role. Someone in the casting department sure messed things up.

§

Since Gil and I testified, Ainsley got final argument, and he capitalized on all the advantages of recency. Local court observers noticed that "young Dunn" used his father's familiar tropes in closing: "Ladies and gentlemen, you're getting ready to go back into the truth chamber. That's what a jury room really is. Back there, it doesn't matter if you personally like the defendants and don't like what you know about Eric Crowder. It doesn't matter if you prefer their lawyers to me. And it doesn't matter if their lawyers are better and more experienced than me. All of that is irrelevant when you enter the truth chamber. The *only* thing that matters in there is what you actually think happened on January 16th. A man was found dead on his own front lawn with his skull crushed in. So what are you going to do to right this wrong? Is justice going to prevail?"

Ainsley paused and picked up the tire iron. He slowly and repeatedly slapped it into the palm of his hand as he continued to speak.

"One blow was not enough to satisfy the hatred in Mr. Merritt's heart. Nor two, or even three. No, he struck the victim four times in the head. *That* is malice. *That* is murderous rage. In the truth chamber, there's no such thing as just letting this one slide. It doesn't get more *real* than this. Everything else gets stripped away and you're left face-to-face with the loss of a human life. You have a very serious decision to make. You know what happened. Listen to your hearts and minds."

Then he very carefully placed the tire iron back onto the evidence table using both hands, as if it were a priceless museum piece.

"Don't be fooled by the smoke screens of a crafty lawyer like Mr. Mobley. He's the best, there's no question about it. But that doesn't mean his client is innocent. You know the truth. You know the right thing to do. Remember that we live in a civilized society and you jurors are the gatekeepers of that society. It is an awesome responsibility. On behalf of the state of South Carolina and the county of Logan, I respectfully ask that you find these men guilty of murder, because they *are* guilty. And we've proven it *beyond* a reasonable doubt."

Ainsley followed his daddy's script verbatim. Big Bill would have been proud.

Chapter 23

Judge Sumwalt's jury instructions lasted almost an hour. When our jury went out to deliberate at a little before noon on Friday, Gil and I were led back to holding cells adjacent to the courtroom. A deputy took our belts and neckties to keep us from hanging ourselves.

The same deputy brought us a lunch, but we had no appetite. Around 3:15, our lawyers came back and informed us that the jury had sent a note requesting to hear some testimony again. As soon as they left, the deputy brought us our belts and ties, saying, "Here are your nooses back."

Once the jury filed in, the court reporter played back a portion of Ainsley's cross-examination of Gil concerning the limited conversation during which Eric supposedly said he was going to kill Regina. After they listened once, the jury foreman turned around in his chair and looked at several other jurors, all of whom nodded affirmatively. They'd heard what they wanted. The foreman then thanked the judge, and the jury filed back out. They seemed subdued.

Back in the holding cell, as Gil was taking off his tie again, he said, "What do you make of that?"

"I quit trying to predict what jurors were thinking years ago."

"Well try now."

"Obviously, there's some confusion or disagreement about that portion of your testimony."

"You think those people who were nodding are on our side or not? Don't you think they *believe* me?"

"There's no way to know."

"You've been doing this shit how long? Don't you have a feel for it?"

"No." I motioned my head toward the deputy. We didn't need to have this conversation in his presence.

We always knew that everything would come down to whether or not the jury bought our story about what happened at the Lakeside. It was a tough sell, but we hoped it might appeal to the women on the jury. I knew that individual jurors can weigh evidence on separate scales, with emotions, not rationality, sometimes determining guilt or innocence. In order to cheer myself about our prospects, I thought of one of Uncle Robert's favorite aphorisms: "The only concept more subjective than the afterlife is reasonable doubt." He'd always laugh after saying it, as if delivering a punchline.

About 6:00, our lawyers reappeared to inform us that the foreman had sent a note to the judge saying they were hung. Gil was elated, but I knew better. It was only natural that he felt heartened that someone believed us and was willing to stand up to the people on the other side. But I knew that, more often than not, this situation turns out badly for the defense, as hung juries typically are leaning toward conviction. Given the mounting pressures, how long would our juror (or jurors) remain steadfast? Experience told me that one side would eventually capitulate, and that a mistrial was unlikely. I said nothing to Gil, however. I didn't want him freaking out.

Once we were back in session, Judge Sumwalt brought the jury to the courtroom and, over the objections of both defense attorneys, read an instruction called an *Allen* charge. It is used to prevent a hung jury by encouraging those jurors in the minority to reconsider their position: *No juror is expected to give up an honest belief he or she might have as to the evidence; but, after full deliberation and consideration of the evidence in this case, it is your duty to agree upon a verdict if you can do so.*

And, it tells jurors that *they should listen, with a disposition to be convinced, to each other's arguments.* Defense counsel always detests such a charge, believing it causes sympathetic jurors to surrender their beliefs in the interest of judicial economy. In my practice, it led to guilty verdicts ninety percent of the time.

Before he excused them, the judge also told the jurors that they would be put up in a hotel overnight if a verdict couldn't be reached "sometime tonight." This was also inappropriate, I believed, since it put further pressure on them to make a decision.

At 8:30 p.m., as we sat in our cells, the deputy, smiling, told us, "The bailiff said they're yellin' in the jury room. Not sure if that's good or bad for you boys."

I thought about those times in my career when I'd been pleasantly surprised by jury verdicts—cases I had no business winning, but somehow did. It was astonishing, really, how a dozen folks could base an important decision on an illogical premise constructed out of desperation or on some trivial, irrelevant matter that I'd casually thrown in as a red herring, never once believing there was a possibility of its success. Sometimes it came down to salesmanship.

At 11:08, Fred poked his head in the holding cell and said, "They're back."

When Gil and I went in, the gallery was buzzing with anticipation. I was surprised by how many people were still around this late in the evening. All of the exit doors were now occupied by armed deputies. Being inside a courtroom at night always felt odd to me, as if something covert was afoot. In the darkness outside the large windows, I could see one dim streetlight. I very much wanted to be standing under it. Tapping his gavel, Judge Sumwalt said, "Quiet down. Order. The jury has a verdict. Everyone take their seats. Bailiff, bring the jury. Ladies and gentlemen, I don't want any outbursts when the verdicts are read. I want everyone to remain calm and quiet."

As they filed in, no juror looked toward the defense table. The foreman handed the verdict forms to the elderly bailiff, who after seven shuffling steps delivered them to the judge, who read the forms without changing his facial expression. He then gave them to a woman with the Clerk's office, saying "Please publish the verdicts." At that point, it was like being a passenger in a car and realizing it's about to wreck.

Not knowing whose name would be called first, Gil and I stood up together to accept our verdicts, the scraping of our chair legs the only sound in the silent courtroom. My verdict was read first. The clerk stammered over a few words, but she was clear and unequivocal with the essential one. When Eric Crowder's family heard *Guilty* of murder they cheered. The judge tapped his gavel unenthusiastically and said, "Order. Order in the Court." I glanced at Fred's face; he looked sad but not surprised. When Gil's verdict was read, the Crowder clan was ecstatic. Gil turned away from me.

Given a case of this magnitude, Fred asked that the jurors be polled individually. Their names were called and each was required to verbally affirm the verdicts. Then the judge thanked the jurors for their service and said the Clerk of Court would mail them a check. The jury walked out the door. I noticed many of them showed up minutes later at the back of the courtroom to listen to our sentencing. By law, Judge Sumwalt had the option to sentence us either to life without parole or to 30+ years, the latter meaning he could sentence us to 30 years *or* to any number above that, of which we'd serve 85 percent. If he felt like making a statement with his sentence, it could be 100 years.

Sumwalt wanted to hear from the victim's family first. Eric's mother, Inez, gave a rambling, tear-soaked diatribe about how we had tried to besmirch her son's good name with false allegations of spousal abuse. She asked the judge for the death penalty, which Sumwalt explained he didn't have the authority to do. When she called Regina a "lying harlot," Judge Sumwalt very kindly said, "Your daughter-in-law is not before me for sentencing." Eric's father and daughter were more effective, emphasizing their desire for the judge to sentence us to life without parole. "I never want them to see the light of day," his father said.

Ainsley, who hadn't been able to stop smiling since the verdict was read, concluded the State's sentencing presentation:

"Judge, to my mind, the fact that Mr. Merritt is a lawyer makes this case *that* much worse. He knew better. His actions are a stain on our entire profession. We respectfully ask the court for maximum sentencing."

In mitigation, Emily spoke a little about our life together and hedged by saying, "It was perfect until all this happened." She also claimed I was "not a man who goes looking for trouble. He's always avoided confrontation for as long as I've known him. I'm positive he would act only in self-defense." She asked Judge Sumwalt to find it in his heart to be lenient. Her voice trailed off. "He's all I have, Judge." Emily tried to walk over to be by my side, but the deputies politely prevented her from getting any closer than ten feet.

Next, Fred mentioned some of the accomplishments of my law career in an attempt to offset Ainsley's takedown on behalf of our profession. Although knowing it was a waste of time, he briefly addressed the "unusual facts" of the case, saying, "I'm obviously disappointed in the jury's decision, but respect it nonetheless. Of all the cases I've had in my long career, this outcome hurts the worst because I know what a good person this man is. I'll never stop fighting for him in the appellate arena."

Since I was exhausted from the stress of trial, my address to the court may have come across as unemotional. Anger and fear, however, lay just beneath the surface.

"I'm sorry as I can be about what happened to Mr. Crowder, but he left me no choice in the matter. I had to defend myself. Would he be on trial if I was dead? That's what I'm trying to figure out. Would the prosecutor have believed his story, that the unarmed men in his yard posed a mortal threat to him? Would anybody have wondered why we were there in the first place? Would the truth of the events leading up to this struggle ever have been known to the prosecution? My gut instinct is that the answer to these questions is "no" and that I would have suffered an unjustified, misunderstood death. No one would've known we were trying to help a woman we *thought* was in grave danger. Eric Crowder lured us over there so he could get away with killing us on his own property. And unfortunately for me, that means I'm getting ready to be sentenced for murder."

Next, Chad Hollingsworth spoke about Gil's writing career. The way he went on, you would've thought Faulkner was his client. I think even Gil was embarrassed by it. I knew Chad was trying to earn his money after a devastating loss, but nothing mattered now.

Though Regina had offered, Chad and Gil had enough good sense not to have her speak during the sentencing phase, which in addition to looking bad, would've made the Crowder family apoplectic. Instead, for the female perspective, Gil's ex-wife Hannah was enlisted to say some good things about him: his strict work ethic as a writer, his compassion for the underdogs of society, his intolerance of injustice, especially when the powerful took advantage of the powerless. For a minute there, I thought she was talking about his father.

Hannah, her hair pulled back in a tight bun, had dark circles under her eyes. As she spoke, I couldn't help but glance at Regina. I wondered what she must be thinking about Hannah's poise and eloquence. When she finished speaking, Gil softly thanked her. It didn't matter that her words were part fiction; this was Hannah's final gesture of love.

Charlie Reese spoke next. After detailing their lifelong friendship, he described Gil as "brilliant" and said that "the verdict today is a horrible miscarriage of justice and has left a hole in my heart that can never be repaired." He introduced his wife Maggie, saying she was "too devastated to address the court because Gil has been like a brother to her."

When the judge asked Gil if he had anything to say on his own behalf, he said, "Nothing. It's been said."

I'm proud to say that neither Gil nor I stooped so low as to enlist any preachers to speak on our behalves, a strategy many think will somehow help them in sentencing. It doesn't, even if it's someone sincere like Miguel. Judges don't put any stock in what preachers say during mitigation. Criminal court is no place for redemption.

Before handing down his sentence, Judge Sumwalt lectured me about being a poor representative of the legal profession, just as Ainsley had. Revealing that he believed my case was entirely about revenge, he said, "I understand the situation with your dog, Mr. Merritt. But I would expect a lot more impulse control and maturity from a member of the Bar. You should have just reported the man if you thought it wasn't an accident. Lawyers should trust the legal process." Then he gave me life in prison.

He turned to Gil. "Mr. Hampton, I didn't know your father but I'm aware that he was a highly respected member of the Bar, which makes your presence before me all the more baffling. I know you were raised better. This was all so senseless. Some cases I still don't understand after hearing all the evidence, and this is one of them. I don't need to tell you how many great works of literature explore the tragic consequences of adulterous behavior. When you're confined to the penitentiary for the rest of your natural life, maybe you'll have time to revisit some of those classics."

It was bush-league for Sumwalt to bring Uncle Robert into it, and for a moment I worried that Gil might have a withering response, but he remained silent. I was relieved. Appellate courts don't take kindly to defendants who lash out at the judiciary. Sumwalt hammered his gavel. "Deputies, take the prisoners. This case is concluded."

For everyone's safety, the cops quickly escorted us away. Convicts are not allowed to touch their family. When I looked over at Emily on the way out, her head was down, her hair covering her face like a curtain.

Detective Garrett seemed to enjoy hauling Gil away. Without the benefit of handcuffs, it would've been one hell of a contest between those two. That was the last time I saw Gil. Co-defendants are separated immediately. He was taken directly to a paddy wagon with two other prisoners and driven to Columbia, while I spent the night in the local jail with no visitors allowed except lawyers. I was transported the next morning.

When Fred came to see me, he apologized repeatedly for the outcome of the case, which he didn't have to do. It wasn't his fault. I understood all too well that the obligatory visit to a recently convicted client is one of the most difficult things a lawyer ever has to do. I didn't mention how disappointing it was not getting at least a verdict of voluntary manslaughter. He knew.

It got to be late and Fred seemed to be lingering for no other reason than concern about my welfare. He was obviously drained, his clipped trial voice slipping back into his natural drawl. To release him, I offered my hand.

"Thanks for everything you did," I said. "Now go home to your family. I'm fine, Fred, really. Emily has the money for the appeal."

"You know this isn't over, Jack."

"Right."

"I mean it. There are two or three viable issues."

"I know. You're right."

On his way out, Fred spoke with the desk officer.

"You tried a good case, Mr. Mobley."

"Thanks, Willie. How's your momma doin'?"

"Good. She's gettin' married again."

"She's a fine looking woman. Who's the lucky fella?"

§

That night, alone in the holding cell, I fully understood that my fate had been *right there* since I was a boy. Like the family dog barking at unseen predators in the woods, a voice had warned me. It was the voice of caution and reason and moderation, protecting me, keeping me safe. But what I realized, sitting there in the middle of the night in a space haunted by prisoners from the past, was that I had known all along I would one day ignore that voice at Gil's urging. Destiny—patient, confident—had only to wait me out.

§

At dawn the next day, I was placed in a sheriff's vehicle for transport to Columbia. I was escorted by two young, buzz-cut deputies carrying assault rifles and wearing bulletproof vests. One sat in the back beside me.

The whole way down to Congaree they played country music, which seemed appropriate for the circumstances except it was some of that really bad pop shit. I asked if they had any George Jones and they said no. Fucking rednecks. No Possum.

Chapter 24

Today is my birthday. In one of Congaree's modest attempts to boost morale, inmates' birthdays are acknowledged on the bulletin board, which is decorated with a festive blue cardboard banner. Since I am the only person here born on November 19, I get the banner all to myself: *Happy Birthday Jack Merritt!* The celebration was understated. Not everyone has a big bash like Scripts. Gifting between inmates is not allowed (Reg. 16) since it could be used to deliver contraband. Nevertheless, Easy Ed has given me what he promises is some excellent dope from Colorado, with the tantalizing name *Night Vision*. I didn't have the heart to tell him that I'm abstaining these days.

Emily sent me a birthday card in the mail again this year. "Hope you're hanging in there. Good luck with the appeal. Emily," it read in its entirety. No "love." Still more than I deserve. Needless to say, Gil never remembers anybody's birthday. I did receive a letter from him today, coincidentally, but he wrote only about himself for six pages. He mailed it weeks ago, the prison mail system being notoriously slow. He concluded with "I know you read my letters, so why no response? How old are you, ten?"

Booker asked my age. "That's 'bout when I got me some wisdom. You do the same," he said. Panic made it a point to tell me his granddaddy was fifty-three when he died. This afternoon, Beef said he just saw my name on the bulletin board and he'll ask his wife to make a derby pie for me in the next few days. That was the highlight of my day. I've written her thank-you notes in the past for the goodies she's made. My grandmother taught me to show appreciation through the written word.

§

Skunk found out today that he lost his state court appeal, which I helped with. At the outset, I'd told him that there was "very little chance" of his case being overturned so he wouldn't have unrealistic expectations. Still, the finality is devastating. An inmate in Unit 3 killed himself last month when his appeal was denied. He ate his Order, literally chewed the papers up and swallowed them. He developed a gastric obstruction that, several painful days later, killed him. "Free at last," Booker said. It was a gruesome reminder of the disorienting effect of losing one's appeal.

Skunk, thankfully, doesn't seem like the suicidal type, but you never know what a man's thinking when he's low. His case actually did have a serious evidentiary issue that the Court of Appeals could have considered. But in my experience their rulings are "result-oriented," meaning Skunk would've stood a better chance had his charge been a misdemeanor. Everybody knows that murder cases get overturned as a result of only the most egregious errors, and sometimes not even then, depending on the makeup of the court. Appellate courts are very fond of the concept of "harmless error."

In private practice, I would sometimes avoid facing disappointed clients and their families after they'd received bad news. They needed time to cool off, even if they didn't know it. I would have my paralegal Gwen make up elaborate excuses why I couldn't see them. The worst thing about being a jailhouse lawyer is there's no way to make yourself scarce at a time like this. Skunk is on the same meal schedule as me, so I'll see him three times a day. There is nothing I can say other than abandon all hope, so I'll just listen sympathetically, which is a cultivated skill.

There is still no word on my own appeal. It's going on two years now. They're taking their sweet time with it. But you can't read anything into that as you sometimes can with jury verdicts. I know it's a matter of when the law clerks can finish writing it.

§

I'm more homesick than usual this week. I've been thinking a lot about the farm. As a kid I used to find all sorts of things washed up on the riverbank along the property, most of it trash. How many counties had these items passed through on their way to the farm? How much rain did it take to bring them to me?

The Catawba River rises in the Blue Ridge Mountains of North Carolina and flows into South Carolina beside our farm, afterward becoming the Wateree River thirty miles downstream before arriving in the Congaree National Park less than a mile east of the prison in which I am now discarded.

§

I miss Miguel.

He firmly believes the events and people in our life cohere, somehow make sense.

I, unfortunately, see life as random, messy, plotless. I find no logic in all this chaos. It's the only conclusion supported by the facts.

Spiritual people witness coincidences in life and see the workings of God and, dismissing logic, blindly look for explanations. Yet I see why so many inmates turn to God, for by seeking salvation they find hope. I am an atheist, so I don't even have the comfort of blaming God for my circumstances. It all falls back on me, and I am an abyss.

§

Panic is someone who knows how to get things. And that's exactly why he's spearheading my efforts to find a weapon. On the yard today, he strolled over and unexpectedly placed a phone in my right hand. I was hoping it would be a shiv.

"It's got a few minutes left. Late birthday gift, but you didn't get it from me," he said laughing, then walked away.

It was a cheap burner, the kind drug dealers use for a day and then ditch so they won't be detected. I made sure no guards were watching, confirmed the phone was off, then slid it beneath my waistband.

Phones are much-coveted contraband in the Unit. I'm truly moved by Panic's generosity, because no one's ever given me one before. Such a high-value gift is a sign of true friendship. I've overheard long conversations with wives, family members, lovers, drug dealers, gang members, and lawyers, but I haven't held a phone since the day I was convicted. Possession of this type of contraband (non-weapon, non-narcotic) gets you a week in the hole. Automatic, no appeal.

I didn't want Panic to think I was unappreciative, but the phone was wasted on me because I don't have anyone to call. Since Emily's out of the picture, that only leaves my attorney Fred to call about the appeal. As a lawyer, I hated it when clients would continually bug me about something I had no control over. When the Court of Appeals schedules a hearing, I trust Fred to notify me promptly.

So Panic wouldn't hear that I gave his phone to someone else, I discretely placed it inside an empty Fritos bag and dropped it into a trash can. It was easier than explaining to him that I had no one to call. That would trouble Panic.

§

The figures are in. According to the *State* newspaper, the number of South Carolina prison deaths (state and federal) increased for the fifth consecutive year. All categories rose: Natural deaths were up by 9%, homicides by a startling 23%, suicides by 17%, and accidents by 3%. A prison official was quoted as saying, "The increase in homicides was primarily due to overcrowding, and that's an issue our politicians are going to have to address in the future." The article gave no clarification of what was classified as an accident, which I think was a mistake given that it will lead to conspiracy theories among inmates. The number of escapes also increased for the first time in seven years, from 2 to 5.

On the yard yesterday, after watching me gaze at the wall, Booker said, "Them boys that tries and escape don't care if they live or die. How 'bout you, Jack?"

I only know of three of my clients who died in prison, though I'm sure more have. You lose track of them once they're on the inside, unless you know the family. The only one murdered was Hank Cranfill, who was taken out by Skull and Bones. The other two were old. One died of lung cancer, the other of congestive heart failure, their official COD "natural causes."

I had several who were stabbed or severely beaten, but they all lived, whether they wanted to or not.

§

I've changed my mind about not telling the guards I'm in danger. Constant thoughts of box cutters and shivs have heightened my paranoia. I concluded that I need as many sets of eyes as possible. On Friday, as I was sweeping on the west corridor, I saw Hawk and Troll walking by. The only other person around was Booker, sweeping farther down the hall. It was the perfect time to approach them.

Both seemed concerned for my safety and assured me that they'd try to protect me. Hawk promised to monitor the Skins closely and Troll said he'd let me know if he heard or saw anything suspicious. They advised me to tone down the smart-ass comments.

Shaking his head, Troll said, "The crazy thing is that I've been here twenty years and never *known* a snitch. What's the upside for somebody in the long run, when you're doing life? They've gotta live with the other inmates, not us."

Hawk said, "The best thing to do, Jack, is put an end to this just like it started, through word of mouth. *Reliable* word of mouth. You're not a drug snitch so that shouldn't be too hard. The bigger issue we got is those Skinheads don't like you because you side with the Firm. When it's a racial thing, you never know what's gonna happen next. We'll figure this thing out. I need to think on it awhile." Hawk patted me on the back, which I hoped no one saw.

Then Troll and Hawk went over and talked to Booker for a little bit. I couldn't make out what they were saying, but I heard Booker's response because he's half-deaf and talks so loud: "He gone be awright. Yes, sir. We gonna take *good* care of Jack. You betcha." I love that man.

Chapter 25

Miguel apologized for missing our last session due to the birth of his grandson. It was nice to see him again. He insisted on showing me pictures of "not so little Roberto," 9 lbs., 6 oz.

"Good thing he doesn't have your hairy eyebrows," I said.

"Yet."

"When will Roberto be baptized?" I asked.

"Three weeks from this Sunday."

"Will you perform the ceremony?"

"Oh yes," he smiled, not bothering to cover his teeth. "A glorious day for our family! Everyone is coming, even my sister from Mexico and her five children."

"You think you can help me get a day pass out of here so I can attend as a family friend. Maybe talk to Hawk. I think a service like that would really help my Christian development."

"Ah. You will do anything to get out of prison, even sit through a ceremony that you believe is nothing more than superstition."

"Does it matter whether or not I really believe in the reason for the celebration? Isn't it enough that I'd like to see you and your family be happy with your new grandson."

"No, it is not enough. To *fully* participate in the celebration you must understand it, and that means believing in the Lord."

I could tell he was dwelling on happier matters, aware that we would soon be talking about the depressing topic of Lizzie's death. I knew that Hawk had told Miguel about Lizzie and the circumstances surrounding that night. I finally brought up the subject because I wanted to apologize for not doing enough to protect him and to let Miguel know how sorry I felt about everything. In attempting to explain what happened, I found myself repeatedly saying "I was misled." I know our meetings are confidential, and I trust Miguel, but I didn't feel comfortable using any names since contraband was involved.

Miguel said, "It is sad when someone feels so much guilt that they want to take their own life. Brian was not beyond the Lord's forgiveness. No one is. But he could not see that. There was nothing you could do, Jack."

"The drugs didn't help," I said.

"I have three friends who did peyote in the desert under the stars. They each had a mystical experience that brought them closer to their God. Two are now priests. They feel they're better off from the experience. No one but his Maker can know what young Brian felt that night. It was a matter of free will."

"Do you ever wonder if your God sometimes saves people from suffering?" I asked. "Maybe, just once in a while, do you think He spares someone the pain of death? Like the lady who throws herself from a skyscraper? Do you think God intervenes and takes her soul before she lands? Or passengers in a plane about to crash, before the impact?"

Miguel suddenly stopped scratching his beard and said, "My friend Jack, you're not thinking about hurting yourself, are you?"

"No. Of course not," I said, surprised he thought I would consider such a thing. "I was thinking about Lizzie and his situation, banging his head against that toilet. Do you believe God ended Lizzie's pain at that moment?"

"I believe in the possibility of a lot of different things. Because Jesus had to endure every moment of the pain of his crucifixion, it could be that we, sometimes, are granted a reprieve from ours. But we cannot know, can we?"

"But if it's granted only occasionally, that wouldn't be fair, would it? How can a supreme being be arbitrary?"

"You are trying to out-lawyer religion today, Jack. Is that because you are angry?"

"Probably."

"You know it will do you no good to be angry. Whether you turn it inside or out, you will be unhappy. Dissatisfied. What happened to Brian was not your fault."

I considered telling Miguel about my current safety fears but I didn't want him to think I was in any way blaming him for this mess. How could anyone foresee that my attempt to protect Lizzie would result in the Skinheads calling me a snitch? I hope no one tells him about the incident with Brick. I don't want Miguel worrying about me.

I needed to talk about something other than Lizzie, so I changed the subject to an issue that I'd been struggling with for quite a while. I would've discussed it with Miguel last time if he hadn't cancelled.

"Since I don't believe in an afterlife, it's making my sentence that much more difficult."

"It would."

"The thing is, I don't want to talk myself into something for the wrong reason. It has to be rational. Like you pointed out, I'm still thinking like a lawyer. It's a bad habit."

A quizzical look flashed across Miguel's face. I could tell he wanted me to say more. When I didn't, he said, "That must be unpleasant for you."

"What? Always thinking like a lawyer?"

"No, resisting eternal salvation."

"If I don't win my appeal," I said, "I don't know what I'm going to do."

Miguel slid an index finger inside his orange croc and scratched his foot, then said, "Imagining you win your appeal is something to look forward to, yes?"

"I'm not getting my hopes up. At this point," I said, "I'm focused on avoiding crushing disappointments."

"Is that why you isolate yourself?" Miguel asked.

"From God, you mean?"

"No, no. You've said you don't believe in Him. I'm talking about your family, Jack. You never write your cousin back and you told your wife not to visit anymore. Is it to prove that you don't need anyone? That you can go it alone? What if your cousin quit writing *you*? What would you do then?"

"Don't forget my sister. I don't talk to her either."

"I feel privileged that you visit me, Mr. Merritt," Miguel said, extending his arms outward in a welcoming manner. "I am your friend but I am not your family. Only the Lord can fill that void."

As I stood to leave, Miguel handed me a brown paper bag containing the books he'd gotten for me. I give him more than enough money to make these purchases, knowing that some of them would have to be special ordered. In the past, for his time and trouble, I've tried to get him to keep the change, but he won't hear of it. "Preachers are not waiters," he said, "We don't expect tips. When your appeal wins, you can take me out to my favorite restaurant. Best enchiladas in town. Then you can tip big because my niece is the waitress."

Beef showed up punctually to take me back to the cell and, per procedure, had to search through my three new books. When I am through with these, I'll donate them to the library, where they'll most likely go unread, unless Ed wants to try one.

"I read this and liked it," Miguel said, pointing to *West With The Night*. "Those descriptions! I felt like I was in the cockpit with her."

I figured that Miguel, out of curiosity, might one day get around to reading some of my requests.

"How did you like the part about the dog?" I asked.

"Very true. I see why you like this book. I want to talk about it next time."

Miguel knows about what happened to Chief. I've read him the parts of my transcript where the State establishes his death as my motive. But he hasn't heard the whole story yet, since my explanations to him have always been consistent with the self-defense strategy of trial. I guess I don't want Miguel to know I'm really guilty and have that fact change the nature of our relationship. Or does he already suspect the truth?

Thanking him again, I handed Miguel some cash and a slip of paper with next month's book list, which included Flannery O'Connor's *Collected Stories*. I was eager to see if he would confront the gothic mysteries of his fellow Catholic.

Beef came over and cuffed me.

"Goodbye," I said as we started walking down the corridor. Miguel was already greeting a penitent.

Back in the Unit, Panic told me he heard a rumor that some box cutters got through at shipping and receiving. The story was repeated at dinner by several others, but no one knew the exact number of cutters or who's presently in possession of them, i.e., they aren't sure if any of the Skins have one. Panic, Easy Ed, and Big C assured me that they'll be quizzing their usual contacts. I emphasized that I really needed a weapon.

"I'm on it," Panic said. "Don't worry."

"Just keep telling me that," I said.

Chapter 26

I saw a hawk kiting in the wind, beak to the breeze, seemingly motionless for seconds. Its sudden plunge toward the prison yard ended fifty feet above me. Not slowing, it began a sharp ascent, the tilted tail flashing copper in the sun.

Then the guards called us in.

§

At lunch, over chicken and dumplings, Ed told me "Master says they'll try to come at you on the yard. The rec room's too risky right now."

"When?"

"We don't know everything yet."

I sensed determination in the way he said "yet," but what I needed even more than information was a very sharp blade. There are metal detectors located outside the dining hall, the rec room, the doors to each cell block, and the door to the yard, making it difficult to carry any metal shiv from one sector to the next. Normally, you would need the help of at least one other inmate to get it through, or a guard who's either inattentive or on the take. One problem is that the guards I've befriended are all honest. They'd probably shoot someone trying to stab me, but they wouldn't break the rules to help me get a shiv for protection.

My EpiPen might come in handy. When I first arrived, the guards would see its bulge in my chest pocket and frisk me for contraband, but now they know what it is and they trust me. So, I could try to put a small shiv in my pocket also, and then quickly walk through a check. But I'm hoping I don't have to try this. Panic has promised he's working on the details, and I trust him with my life.

§

My grandfather loved horses. At age 10, he watched the town livery stable burn down. The firemen and townsfolk tried in vain to save the horses. When I first heard this story, I was also ten and already in love with horses. I suddenly understood how Grandad, a force of nature, could be brought to tears. He said the unearthly sounds of their suffering and the smell of their burning flesh never left him. When his mother had to burn the clothes he was wearing because nothing would take out the smell, he panicked, frightened that the fire she'd set would get out of control.

I never lost my fear of fire. So on Tuesday, when I overheard two inmates plotting to create a trash fire as a diversion so they could get to someone, I said, "What if it gets out of control and the sprinkler system fails? We're trapped *underground* here, guys. Is that really how you want to go?"

They told me to fuck off and accused me of being friends with their intended target, which was untrue.

"I don't care about him," I said. "I care about not *burning* to death in a goddamn fire. You're smarter than that, I hope." They appeared to be unmoved.

Three days on, there's been no fire.

§

Today on the yard, I saw a dew-covered spiderweb sparkling in the sun. You cannot stop searching for beauty, or you will perish.

§

Another sun-bright day on the yard. I saw a flash of metal moving quickly toward me. Certain it was a shiv, I flinched before raising my arms, my fists clenched. Then I realized it was only the glint from Beef's clipboard. So I wouldn't look scared or crazy, I pretended to be shadow-boxing, joking around with Beef.

Outside of my close inner circle, I feel like I don't know who is and isn't a Skinhead anymore. I used to be able to tell, or thought I could. Now, wherever I am—the cafeteria, the rec room, the yard—I scan the white guys to see if they're coming for me. Such concentration exhausts me. It's weird being suspicious of your own race.

I've noticed that black inmates who hail from the country call me "cuz" and those from the city call me "homey" or "homes."

All of the Hispanics call me "Miguel's amigo." That's my favorite. Skinheads just call me "nigga lover."

§

The future of the farm is uncertain. My sister wrote to tell me that an outside developer has made an offer on the buildings and land. I know what this means. If sold, the family house will be bulldozed to make way for a new plant—chemicals, plastics, metals. The farm's ponds are ready-made waste reservoirs. Given the location, the labor will be cheap and the officials compliant. It all rides on our appeals. If we lose, I will have to agree to sell. My sister deserves her inheritance. But the assholes will have to pay top dollar for my fish.

The farm holds very little sentimental value for Gil. I'd resented him moving into our grandparents' house when he came back South. I had been responsible for its upkeep since his mother died in 1997, which meant I paid the property taxes, power bills, and maintenance charges, all the mundane yet necessary stuff that no one expects the artist in the family to do. I also looked after the farmland—fencing, bush-hogging, and wildlife management. The work relieved stress, but the job was too big for one person and I was always searching for competent, reliable workers to help me out. Just keeping Grandad's timber-frame barn habitable for horses was work enough.

Gil rarely came home. While he was busy checking out exhibits at the Whitney and MoMA, I was doing everything to preserve some semblance of our shared heritage. The extent of his curiosity about the farm was casually asking every few years, "Seen any big turkeys? I might bring some buddies down." This usually coincided with his befriending an editor or publisher who enjoyed both hunting and bourbon. More often than not they drank until dawn, shouting their favorite James Dickey lines across the restless pond. Following his divorce, he didn't bother coming at all.

After Aunt Betsy died, no one lived at the farm for fifteen years because Gil was up North, my sister Rachel lived out West, and Emily wanted to remain in our house in town. "I prefer to live in my *own* home and not someone else's," she said. The real reason, I believe, was that the country house's many bedrooms would've magnified the absence of children. I tried my best to convince her to move, emphasizing that we could save money since most of the expenses would be paid for by my grandfather's testamentary trust that was set up to maintain the place, a fact which played no small part in Gil's decision to move back.

On those occasions when Gil had visited, he seemed about as interested in his lodgings as he would've been in a Holiday Inn. He was even strangely detached from the library, which I'd always thought of as something of a shrine to Gran. But once he moved in, you would've thought he'd been appointed head librarian. He immediately began cataloguing and taking note of first editions and rarities. He consolidated his own collection of books with Gran's. Based on his lack of literary output in recent years, I had no idea Gil could be that industrious and resourceful. Predictably, there were far too many volumes for the library shelves to accommodate and Gil's project spilled over into all of the bedrooms, the result being I could no longer easily find books I was looking for. Nothing seemed to be alphabetized by author or categorized by genre. It was a system only he understood, a metaphor for his life.

Gil was very pleased with himself when he discovered some of Gran's unpublished poems in a folder on the bookshelf behind Churchill's *World War II*. To honor Gran's memory, Gil decided to self-publish her collected works in a small volume to be available for family and friends. I was disappointed that I hadn't found the poems in the first place, but it was a nice gesture. On January 18, 2012, one hundred copies of the *Collected Poems of Josephine Faircloth* were delivered from Brooklyn to the farm, but Gil was not there to receive the shipment. Like me, he was in the Logan County Detention Facility awaiting a bond hearing on his murder charge. It was not the best way to honor our grandmother.

§

Panic has good news. "We gotcha all set with a shiv, big guy. Handmade special for you. It'll be by the fence in the corner where they didn't weed eat."

"You're positive?"

"*It'll be there.* Count on it."

"We need to make sure all our people know not to move it if they see it," I said anxiously.

"Me and Ed done done that. You think you're dealin' with a bunch of fuckin' amateurs?"

"No boxcutters available?"

"Man, this is much better'n a boxcutter any day. The blade's a lot bigger and just as sharp. Hitler won't know what the fuck hit him."

§

Cold weather came early. The temperature dropped forty degrees in thirty-six hours, unheard of around here. The sky is gray and heavy with moisture. My teeth ache. All inmates have been outfitted with heavy denim coats with a thin lining, compliments of a deal struck between the

DOC and the Salvation Army, according to Booker. They don't keep you warm. This winter must be a trial run. If a bunch of us catch pneumonia, they'll probably keep the coats and make them official winter wear.

A light snow begins as we're leaving the yard. The whirring of the wind-driven flakes could easily lull one to sleep.

§

I came back to my cell, washed my face, and lay down for a nap. Soon I was dreaming again about Emily in Charleston:

It is a clear day and she is standing on the promenade at the Battery as sailboats dot the harbor. In the distance I can make out Fort Sumter. The experience is so vivid that I can taste and feel the salty wind. My mouth waters and my eyes tear. Emily is looking out at the water in anticipation. She is wearing her wedding dress, but it is black.

The only other person on the promenade is five yards in front of her. It is a child, seated at an easel painting an oil portrait of Emily. Emily is unaware of the little girl, whose small legs dangle below the canvas. I never see her face. I do know that the child is *ours*.

The girl meticulously darkens Emily's dress. It is excruciating for me to watch the application of the black paint. Small, delicate fingers wrap around a slowly moving paintbrush. Emily's face, masterfully rendered, is hopeful and expectant. But I know it is false hope.

Our child, left-handed like Emily, finishes the painting in the same way in every dream, with two flourishes: a thin line of black paint on the bridge of Emily's nose for her stitches and a dab of light brown paint on the neck for her birthmark. The painting and the dream are complete.

When I wake up, I am exhausted, spent. I am also relieved that I no longer have to worry about what might occur in the dream, even though it always ends the same way.

Chapter 27

Fifty ankle chains clanking on concrete.

We are proceeding along the southwest corridor on our way to the yard. Normally, the next hour would be the most relaxing part of my day, enjoying a couple of smokes and being outside. But not today.

The steel door slowly grinds open, its rollers high-pitched, irritating, like Miles Davis's missed note at 2:10 into "So What." A bad sign? One imperfection can't ruin a masterpiece, but a single fuck-up can destroy your whole life.

We walk out into blinding silver light, squinting in unison. The weather is much warmer; the snow has melted. The guards said we didn't need coats. It will be easier to maneuver without one.

Our wrist chains are cuffed in front so we can smoke. We're allowed to have one cigarette behind each ear but no packs since they can be used to carry drugs and small weapons like blades. Bumming and trading of smokes is allowed.

I am surrounded by friends in a loose, informal cordon. Booker, Torch, and Big C are still talking about an NFL game's controversial pass interference call that they vehemently disagree with. Easy Ed is complaining to me about the cafeteria changing its brand of canned corn. Panic is telling Master and Fleet about his poker winnings and the IOUs he expects to collect. Panic fumbles, then drops his unlit cigarette by the fence corner, bending down to find it in the tall grass.

Two Skins, Badger and Drip, are at three o'clock talking to each other. A third is at eight o'clock, alone, with his back to us.

As promised, Beef casually weaves his way through the Skins, looking for anything suspicious, like a quick hand-to-hand exchange or a bulge in clothing that could be a weapon.

As Panic brags about all the money he used to win playing cards in the Army, he shields himself behind Torch and places the shiv in my left hand. Fleet tells Panic "that's a lot more jack" than he ever made dealing drugs. I place packets of sunflower seeds on top of the shiv. It is made of a single piece of steel that is both sharp and pointed. The blade is large. The handle feels like it was rounded off by a hammer.

I see some sparrows on the ground searching for food. I excuse myself from talking to Ed and walk toward the birds. I'm in the habit of throwing out seeds for them and they anticipate my daily arrival.

I glance over at Ed who, ever so slightly, shakes his head negatively. Then Ed talks to Booker, who looks at me and also shakes his head, not so subtly. I have them spying on different Skins. No movement. All's calm for now.

Booker is looking old to me today. The lines on his face are accentuated by the slanting afternoon sunlight. I know he's very worried about the threats.

The sparrows flutter their soft brown wings in excitement. They don't fight over food as aggressively as hummingbirds or blue jays, but they are by nature greedy, quick, and opportunistic.

"Who's got the lighter?"

"C."

"When's movie night?

"Dunno."

"What's today?"

"Thursday."

"I mean the date."

"No clue."

"The nineteenth."

"Is that all?"

"Movie night's next week."

I feel like I've got too damn much going on with my hands. Why in the world am I using my right hand to feed birds and smoke when the shiv needs to be in *that* hand? I stand behind Ed and carefully move the shiv to my right hand.

Beyond the fence, on the roof of Unit 4, there are five workmen from Duke Energy wearing yellow hard hats. They are standing in a circle, probably discussing how they'd hate to get stuck in this goddamn place.

A cloudless sky. What I took for a bird turns out to be a distant twin-engine plane. My vision has gotten worse. Why the hell did I forget my glasses?

I notice one of the sparrows is wounded. What I had thought was dirt is actually dried blood from a tiny, vertical cut. Probably nicked the wire.

I hear workmen on the roof laughing. There is nothing inmates resent more than seeing outside folks enjoying themselves. As I look up, one of them tosses a cigarette down into the shrubbery.

I eat some sunflower seeds, then kneel down to get a look at the bird's wound, emptying my bag onto the ground to coax it nearer. It is tentative, unsure.

Suddenly Booker screams my name. Startled birds scatter.

Acknowledgments

Special thanks to my editor Tom Rash. The best advice I can offer any aspiring writer is to find an editor who's three times smarter than you.

My appreciation to Emöke B'Racz, founder of Malaprop's Bookstore, who knew exactly how to motivate me with just one sentence (our secret).

My gratitude to novelist Tommy Hays for his kindness and encouragement as a teacher and to the Great Smokies Writing Program.

Thanks to the following for their close readings and suggestions: May Rhea, Tom and Camille McKinney, Carolyn Begley, Beth Branham, Philip Clarke, K-Bob ("less is more"), Catherine Darby, Bill Barrier, Lucy Cobos, Patricia Anastasi, Van and Candace Talbert, Judge John Hayes, Harry Dest, Leland Greeley, Charlie Burnette, Trez Clarke, Joel Estes, Carolyn Hill, Randy Safer, Kip Pritchard, Frank Robards, Bruce Johnson, Jimmy Burnette, Jeanna Mills, Bill Baggett, Tony Nolan, Pat Kavanaugh, Dennis Kokenes, MD, Dean Secor, Charles Frederick, Jim Cargile, Rebecca Caldwell, Lauren Harr, and Kelly Clayton.

My appreciation to Carter Wood, MD, Eva Sikora, MD, and Leigh Ann Hamon, DVM, for sharing their medical expertise.

Many thanks to the amazing team at Redhawk Publications: Patty Thompson, Robert Canipe, Richard Eller, Tim Peeler, and Erin Mann. Your belief in the book means everything.

I am indebted to the late Jim Hipp, who taught me to love the written word.

As always, I am grateful to John, Mel, and Jerry for a lifetime of unwavering friendship.

About The Author

A former criminal defense attorney, John Rhea graduated from Clemson University and the University of South Carolina School of Law. He lives in the mountains of Western North Carolina with his wife and their three rescue pets. This is his first novel.

johnrheaauthor.com

www.ingramcontent.com/pod-product-compliance
Lightning Source LLC
Chambersburg PA
CBHW020602030726
47497CB00007B/2047

BIBLIOTHÈQUE DE LA JEUNESSE

AVENTURES DU CAPITAINE
COUGOURDAN

PAR EUG. MOUTON

LIBRAIRIE 2f50 HACHETTE

Bibliothèque
des Écoles et des Familles

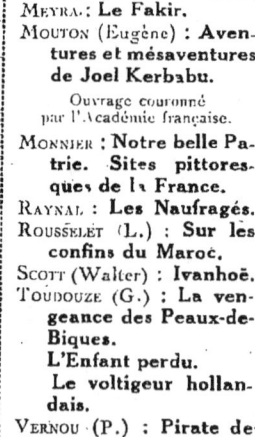
Pour la collection complète,
demander le Catalogue de Distribution de Prix.